# Cherry Blossom Express

Kate Ressman

GOLDEN FLEECE PRESS

Golden Fleece Press
PO Box 1464,
Centreville, VA 20122
www.goldenfleecepress.com

Special discounts are available on quantity purchases by corporations, associations, and others. For details, contact the publisher at the address above.
U.S. trade bookstores and wholesalers please contact Ingram Content Group at customerservice@ingramcontent.com or by telephone at 800.973.8000(option 3).

Epub ISBN 13: 978-1-942195-00-9
Mobi ISBN 13: 978-1-942195-01-6
Print ISBN 13: 978-1-942195-03-0
Pdf ISBN 13: 978-1-942195-02-3


Printed in the United States of America


First Edition


10 9 8 7 6 5 4 3 2 1

To

Dorothy Ressman

who stayed up all night to read the first draft.

# ACKNOWLEDGMENTS

No author truly works alone. So, this book is also the work of Tamela Ritter who gave me good edits and loved my characters; Kim Roper who came to visit me in the madness of the first 72 hours and let me chatter about characters and plots over dinner and copyread the thing; Julia Ehrmantraut who created the cover, fussed with the layout, and generally made the whole story turn into a book; and Ashley Voris who did final checks on all the versions.

To all of you, I say thank you.

And to my parents, who have let me rest in their nest while I get ready to fly and given me nothing but support: Thank you and I love you.

Chapter 1

Iko smoothed down the skirt of her cherry blossom pink dress with one white gloved hand. Her hand trembled. She forced it to stop. The train was starting to fill up around her. She clutched her ticket, crumpling the edge. There was a woman wrapped in fabric across the aisle. She glanced at her and then out the window near her. She didn't want to be rude, even though she wanted to spend more time staring at the fabric. The hand-spun cotton was delicately embroidered with white patterns she couldn't decipher.  The woman in homespun cotton was sitting across from an old military man. He was wearing an impressive red trimmed uniform. He had a large grey mustache that drooped like a cartoon walrus'. His eyes were closed and he was snoring slightly.

Iko twitched her skirt back into place. Her eyes roamed the car. The train-car had three sets of six seats on each side. The red leather seats were facing each other three to three. Wood paneling ran around the lower edge of the car and shining chrome filled the top and ceiling. Red cloth curtains could be pulled across the windows. Most of the windows were open to combat the warmth of the July summer in Washington, DC. The car was almost filled.

A fragile-boned woman was leaning against her husband in the corner farthest away from the first class cars. Her black pants stopped about six inches above her pumps.  Her husband was writing in a small book while she stared out the window. His well-groomed brown beard nearly reached his shirt. Iko's mother would be appalled.

Most of her fellow travelers looked like mass-produced businessmen. One or two of the younger ones gave her an appreciative glance. She instantly dropped her eyes so that she would not to see the looks mutate into something nasty when they noticed the slant of her eyes. She'd had enough of that in high school.

A little boy crawled into the seat next to her. He gave her a gap-toothed smile. "I'm Jimmy." His blond hair was slicked back and parted neatly to the right. He offered a lollipop-sticky hand.

"A pleasure to meet you, Jimmy. I'm Miss Maynard." She shook his hand gently. She didn't mind the red that transferred to her gloves. She could bleach them white at some point.

"Hi, Miss May."

His mother caught up with him a moment later. She was breathing a little quickly and frowning.  Her matching blonde hair was pulled back into a knot at the back of her neck, but a few hairs were slipping free creating a halo around her head as the sun hit her. "What did I tell you about running off?" She offered Iko an apologetic smile. Her dress was simple yellow cotton with white lace trim at the throat and hem.

"This is Miss May." Jimmy gestured grandly at Iko.

"Melissa Wells," the woman offered.

"Iko Maynard." They exchanged polite nods. Melissa sat down next to the window with Jimmy between her and Iko. Jimmy crawled into her lap to look out the window. His white sailor suit looked all the brighter against her skirt. He waved his pinwheel at the passengers on the platform. Iko remembered folding a pinwheel for her little brother. She smiled. She'd colored it with wax crayons to make it like a rainbow when it spun. And he'd spun it with his breath when the wind wouldn't blow. He puffed like a little train engine.

The porter called "All aboard." A sharp whistle pierced the air. With a jolt the train started to move. It shook a bit as it gathered speed.

"Finally," the man sitting across from her muttered. He folded his newspaper into another neat section and bent back to his reading. He'd already worked his way methodically through the first three pages. Iko had glanced at the headlines, they were all about the armistice agreement in Korea. Another war ended in her lifetime. Maybe it actually would be the last. Folding and refolding the paper so that it remained neatly in his space. He kept his long legs tucked up close to his seat.

The man in the center seat stretched his legs out. He crossed them at the ankles, pulled his hat down over his face. He folded long fingers over his stomach and closed his eyes. The young man nearest to the window stared out at the platform. He chewed at his lip and blinked rapidly. Iko felt a surge of sympathy. He was leaving home too or leaving someone behind. She wanted to reach out, find out if he was going all the way to Boston or if he was leaving when they made it to New York City.

The thought made no sense. She didn't know him. She knew nothing about him beyond the fact that he was sitting in a train and chewing on his lip. Settle down, she told herself firmly. There is no reason for you to embarrass yourself. It would be unbearably rude to ask him.

The thought crept up -- you could check his ticket when the porter comes by. She mentally shook herself. Really, what was she thinking?

The military man's eyes opened. He shifted his beach ball of a stomach as he moved. His truly impressive mustache and sideburns were pure grey. "You're from

India then?" he pressed the woman in the white fabric. His accent was British. It suited his booming voice. He had to be nearly seventy.

The woman gave him a polite smile that didn't reach her eyes. "Yes." Her dark hair was coiled up in a long braid that she'd turned into a bun. A scarf draped loosely over her hair in brilliant peacock colors.

"Stationed there, I was. In 1900." He patted his thigh. "Well before this happened. Lovely place." He sighed. "Rather miss the markets. Not the snakes though. Sneaky little critters."

Her smile grew more genuine. "I have never been fond of the snakes myself," she offered. "Where were you stationed?"

They launched into a conversation about wondrous places Iko had never heard of. Mrs. Wells moved to the seat next to Iko. "Jimmy, do not drop that."

"I won't." The little boy seemed to be trying to fit half of his body out of the train window.

"I hope you don't mind. He wanted to look out the window."

"Oh, of course not. My little brother would have done the same. Has done the same."

The train reached its full speed and settled into a soothing repetition of click-clack-click.  It swayed gently from side to side. Iko studied the carpeting. She had a book that her mother had pressed into her hands at the station. She opened her purse and pulled it out. Reading the inside flap, she sighed. As suspected, it was a classic. Something she should read as opposed to anything she'd actually like. Still, her mother had given it to her and there were hours between DC and Boston. She slipped her slightly crumpled ticket into the book and opened to the first chapter.

She was interrupted not a minute later by the arrival of the conductor. The conductor was an older Negro with a neatly pressed uniform of deep blue. His eyes were crinkled up at the corners and his mouth was curled up in an open smile. He took her ticket, punched it, then tucked it into the metal rim above her seat. "The dining car is two cars that way." He pointed in the opposite direction from first class. "They'll be serving lunch from 11 to 2 and dinner from 6 to 9. There will be a coffee and tea cart that comes through at four."

"Thank you," she said, smiling up at him.

Newspaper raised a brow at her and his lips quirked up on one side in a half-hearted smile. He nodded to the conductor and handed over his ticket before he put his head back down to study the intricacies of business or baseball, whichever section he was on now. Iko watched the conductor as he gathered tickets on the other side of the aisle. He had a small limp, but otherwise moved with a practiced grace. She was leery of trying to stand up on the small heels her mother had insisted upon for this trip. She looked down at the two inch heels. She'd seen women wearing heels twice as high getting into the first class section. *I'd break an ankle*, she thought. The train shook and shimmied over some piece of track that wasn't perfectly smooth. The conductor never faltered.

She opened the book once more. It felt thick and heavy in her hands. It smelled faintly of dust from whatever library sale it had come from. The page number mocked her with its unchanging three for nearly fifteen minutes. She couldn't concentrate on it. She closed the book and put it back into her purse. To her surprise a magazine suddenly appeared in her line of view. She turned to see Mrs. Wells smiling at her. "<u>Bleak House</u> is dreadful. I think you might enjoy this. I brought two. We can trade."

"Thank you." Iko took the <u>Life</u> magazine with a smile. She looked over at Jimmy. He was kneeling up on his seat, his arms folded under his chin as he watched the white pinwheel spin and spin in the breeze of the train. If only she could be so easily entertained. The young man across from Jimmy had stopped chewing on his lip. He was staring down at a stack of stationary - love letters, or a novel perhaps. Or maybe something even more interesting. Maybe he was a scientist or a reporter who was studying the secrets of the world.

She lost herself in the world of celebrities and time slipped away. The next stop let three people from the car off. Everyone else seemed to be heading further on to New York or Boston or beyond. Newspaper was nearly done with his paper, she'd have to find something else to call him. He folded the paper into its last eight sections. Iko looked through the car. The sun was glimmering off of the sleek chrome detailing of the side panels. Sparkles of light played across the dark maroon carpet, making it look like it had an actual pattern.

The old British soldier had fallen asleep again. One hand rested on his broad stomach displaying his thick fingers. The other clutched his cane to his side. The little silver dog head peered out between his fingers. The woman in white gave her a polite nod. Iko returned it and let her eyes play further on. The woman who had curled up like a child in her seat was drawing now. She had a thick pad of paper and a stick of charcoal. There was no way of knowing who or what had brought that frown of concentration to her face. She seemed content. Iko couldn't see a wedding ring on her or the man with the beard, but the familiar way they leaned into each other's space made her think they were husband and wife, not brother and sister. They reminded her of her Aunt Marcie and Uncle Simon - wrapped up with each other and unable to understand that other people might not be comfortable with their attentions.

"Your first time on this trip?" Newspaper asked. His voice was soft and light. His eyes were dark and sharp, like a predatory bird. She nodded. He gave her a nod of his own. "Just relax. The line is very reliable."

She gave him a smile. She turned her attention back to the latest fashions – feeling as though she'd just been rebuked for the curiosity that her mother swore would kill her someday.

"Of course, you could try talking to your neighbors." His voice was full of laughter now. "I'm sure that my associate Mr. Gold here, would be glad to talk to you."

Hat, or rather, Mr. Gold, groaned when Newspaper kicked his ankle. "Must you?"

"Always."

Gold resettled himself in his seat and pushed his hat back to the top of his head. "Why hello there. I'm Dom Gold."

"Iko Maynard."

"A pleasure, Miss Maynard. Are you traveling on business or pleasure today?"

"I'm moving to Boston."

"I haven't been to Boston in years," he replied. "Are you going to meet your fiancee?"

Iko's eyes narrowed. "I'm not engaged at this point, Mr. Gold."

Newspaper's lips were curled up at the edges. He was enjoying this. She couldn't tell if her responses were amusing him or if it were Gold's questions. "Wonderful. That means we could have a whirlwind romance on the train and end married by the end of June." Gold's smile was bright, teasing. "Lewis can be our witness." He gestured to Newspaper. "And we can have our young pinwheel wielder carry the rings."

"But Mr. Gold, you've told me nothing about yourself," she returned. "How can I know that you'll make a good husband?"

"I'm neat and earn a steady salary," he informed her. "I am a writer."

"He's a reporter for the *New York Times*," Lewis – was that a first or last name, she couldn't tell – translated.

"I am." Gold's eyes crinkled as he grinned. "And there's nothing quite like it. Is this your first trip to Boston?"

"No, I've been up several times. When were you last there?"

"Oh, goodness. It must have been ten years ago." Gold's eyes got distant. He was seeing someone else in her place. "Yes. Ten years. I was writing a human interest piece, I think. Talking to researchers at the college. And you're moving there. With family?"

She shook her head, suddenly unsure if she wanted him to know that much. "I'll be working at M.I.T."

"Really?"

"Yes, sir." She folded her hands over her purse and told herself to not clench her fingers.

"Let me guess, a new librarian? No, no, not a librarian. I know, you'll be working as a nurse."

She shook her head with a smile and dropped her head to the side. She wanted to know what he would come up with next.

"An assistant to the groundskeeper. No, I have it, you'll be taking over as president." He smiled smugly at her, as though he'd just made the best joke in the world.

She laughed. "I'll be working in the admissions office."

"That was my next guess."

"Weren't we supposed to be stopping at all the stations on this line?" the artist's voice rang out through the train car. It carried with the unconscious training of an actress or singer to hit all the corners. Her companion turned to look at her. Lewis' head turned toward her.

"Yes," he answered. He finished the last page of the paper and tucked it away. "I'm going to clean my hands." He made his way to the lavatory. He walked with steady purpose, not even stumbling when the train jerked forward like it had been a cork stuck in a bottle.

"Well, we just blew through a small station. It was brick and there was a person standing on the platform with bags next to him." She frowned around the cabin. "Where's the conductor?"

Jimmy's pinwheel made a whirring whip of noise in the still car. Iko thought of windmills and the camp in the middle of farm country where she'd been sent as a child with her mother. It made the same sound, speeding up right before storms and when the skies turned to bottle green. She stared at the artist in the corner seat. Gold turned in his seat and leaned forward to catch a look at her. The young woman was frowning, a line forming between her eyes.

Her companion put a hand on her arm. "Calm down, Pam. There was probably no one who needed to stop there. We're making up time for the delays in Richmond." He stroked gently down her arm. "Let's go scrounge some lunch and you'll feel better."

Iko politely averted her eyes from the scene. She didn't want to embarrass the woman. Pam, her mind supplied. Lewis sat back down, giving her something to look at instead. She looked at his suit, a lovely grey pinstripe layered over a white shirt and a pale yellow vest or oriental brocade with a tie of soft blue. A little silver tie bar winked at his throat.

In contrast, Gold's suit was natural linen — a little light for the season -- over a pink shirt and a cream colored vest. His tie was a narrow slice of dark rose silk. He wore a carved onyx and silver ring, heavy and old. It looked like a family piece. A pocket-watch chain winked on his vest. They were both dark haired, but Lewis' eyes were heavy chocolate brown and Gold's a soft grey. Lewis located a book in his leather satchel. The bag didn't match him at all. It was worn brown leather that didn't match his black shoes.

Gold regarded the bag with interest. He poked through it without asking. "Here we are," he said with satisfaction. He held up a pack of cards. "Anyone up for a few hands of bridge? Cribbage? Go Fish?" he asked, eyeing Jimmy. The little boy's eyes widened.

"Oh, may I?" He turned big, blue eyes on his mother. She laughed.

"You may."

"Wonderful." Gold settled himself on the floor in front of his seat. Lewis looked down at him and shook his head. Jimmy sat across from him and they started a rousing game of Go Fish. A glance at Gold's cards showed that he was playing to lose. The second hand had Lewis poking Gold with his toe.

"Deal me in."

The young man in the window seat looked up from his letters. He smiled at the scene. He looked across and met Iko's eyes. He blushed and looked away quickly. His head whipped to the side. "We just passed another station." His voice was thin, like watery oatmeal.

"Maybe it was just a service station?" Mrs. Wells offered.

Iko didn't like the strain in her voice. She sounded close to tears. Iko looked at her in alarm. She put a hand on her wrist when she saw the over-bright eyes. "Melissa?" she dared to use the woman's first name. "Are you alright?"

"I'm fine," she said. She watched the men playing with her son.

Iko read between the lines. "Your husband?"

"Is in Korea," she said quietly. "We're going to stay with my parents for a while."

"I see. I'm sure it will be fine. Jimmy will enjoy seeing his grandparents."

"Yes. He will. He just keeps asking when Daddy will be coming home." Her voice dropped to a whisper. "And I hate to lie to him, but we just don't know. I don't know if he'll be getting any of his leave time this month, armistice or not. I just don't know how to answer the question anymore."

"My mother used to tell me and my brother that it would happen when we least expected it. He would be there like the best surprise in the world. Maybe it would be our birthday, maybe it would be nothing but a stormy sky or maybe it would be when we closed our eyes at night."

"Your father was in the War?"

"Yes. He fought in France." That brought a slight smile to the other woman's face.

She wasn't that much older Iko thought suddenly. There was maybe five years between them. "So did mine. It hurt that he was away for so long, but I think I missed him more than my little brother. I don't think he even remembered Father when he was a child. He was only one when he went away."

"But he remembered and met him later, right?"

"Right."

"And Jimmy remembers his father."

"He does." Iko gave her arm a squeeze. Gold glanced up at her with an approving smile and a nod. She looked down at her magazine. "Did you want to trade now or wait a bit longer? I still have a few articles to read."

"Oh, we can wait. I haven't really been reading." Mrs. Wells smiled then. "I've just been looking at the dresses. The skirts look so full."

"On those new Vogue patterns? Yes, they do. I don't know how you're supposed to sit in one."

"Carefully?" the other woman offered. "I heard you're going to be working at the university? My father teaches there. He's in the math department. Maybe we'll run into each other. We should at least get some coffee. I can show you around the city."

"I'd like that. Thank you. Did you grow up there?"

"I did. It's a lovely place. Have you flown kites? There's an expanse called the commons where you can fly them in the spring. I'm planning to take Jimmy out and hand make a kite or two."

"That sounds like fun. I remember making myself a kite out of sticks and newspapers with my mother. I got glue all over my hands and I had bits of newspaper stuck to the ends of my braids." She got a laugh at that. "It's hard to imagine we were ever that young."

"It is."

"Did you make the pinwheel?"

"Oh, no, there's this man in town who makes children's toys. He gives them out to the kids when they come up to his door. He's somewhere around eighty now. Still the neatest work on the street. He can fix anything. He tells the kids stories of things before the trains and cars and record players. I don't remember a world like that. It's amazing that someone still does."

"My mother always told me that we should listen to our elders not simply because of their age, but because we had never seen what they have seen. I think that's something she learned from her parents."

"We've passed another station. Something is wrong." This time the voice was that of a strident man in the far corner diagonal to where Pam was sitting. "That was my stop. I'm going to find the conductor." He left his newspaper on the seat and left the car. A brief intense noise accompanied him opening the door.

"Now that isn't something you see every day. Do you think we should investigate?" Gold's voice was mild, but he knocked his shoulder into Lewis's knee. They were wedged in between the seats. Jimmy was the only one who looked particularly comfortable down there.

"Yes, I'll go see if I can find out what's happening. Would you be so kind as to play out my hand, Miss Maynard?" Lewis offered her his fan of cards.

"Yes, of course." She took the cards carefully. She was not going to sit on the floor, no matter how clean the carpeting looked. Lewis got to his feet less than gracefully. She dipped her head to hide her smile. Gold outright laughed at him. Lewis kicked him gently in the back as he dusted himself off and straightened his jacket. He took off in the opposite direction. He headed toward the engine. The driver should know what was happening.

"Your turn, Miss May," Jimmy informed her. He wasn't bothered by the missed stations. He had three sets in front of him. Gold had one. Lewis had one in his hand. Her hand now, she guessed.

"Do you have any fours?" The card game kept her mind occupied for a while and it was nice not to be worried about what could be keeping Lewis from returning. Perhaps he hadn't made it all the way to the front car yet. Perhaps he'd found the emergency before he got there and stopped to help. Strident Voice hadn't returned either. Pam and her companion had gone for lunch. There was no reason for them to have returned yet. The train rocked gently from side to side.

"I wonder if it's ghosts," a small, nasal voice said idly. "They're simply making people see stations that don't exist. That could do it. Or it's a joke. Some sort of experiment to see if people start panicking. The girl started it and now she and her friend are hiding out to see how we all react. And they're keeping anyone who leaves from coming back so they don't spoil the observations."

"Could be. But how are they keeping track of what happens inside the car? We'd see them looking in through a window or the door." The answering voice was cultured and also male.

"Simple. They've got a third person in here taking notes. The young man over there with the letters maybe. Or maybe there's someone in the luggage room watching out through a peephole."

The second man chuckled. "You've spent far too much time at the movies," he said. "And far too long with your head stuck in psychology journals. Time to join the real world again. Here. Have the paper. There's a good rundown on the new football teams. You need to know these things so that you can interact with normal people when you get home."

"Very funny." There was a rustle of paper though, so presumably he'd accepted the opportunity to read up on some knowledge he didn't have.

Unlike Lewis and Gold, Iko was willing to challenge Jimmy a bit. She put down two sets, leaving her with three mostly useless cards. Jimmy looked at her suspiciously. He put down another set.

"Do you have any kings?" Gold asked. He was doing a rather spectacular job at throwing the game. She could see from her spot that he didn't have any kings himself. Maybe he just wanted a set of them to complement his set of queens. Lewis returned a few minutes later.

He sat in his seat and stared down at his hands. "I couldn't seem to make it to the engine. I kept being blocked by conductors and first class security. The employees claim we haven't missed any of our scheduled stations. That our friend with the voice was just mistaken. They assured me that there was nothing wrong in the least and heavily encouraged me to get some lunch and return to my seat. "

"And you believe them?"

"Not at all. But perhaps a bit of lunch isn't out of the question. We can kidnap young Mister James and use him to enrapture the ladies of the lunch service, if his mother doesn't mind terribly."

"I'll come with you," Mrs. Wells said firmly. "It starts with cards and then it's smoking and drinking. I don't want my son corrupted."

Gold laughed. "She's got your number, Lewis. I'd be careful."

"Gold," Lewis chided with a poke of his toe. "I'm not the one who started playing cards. At least it wasn't the magic tricks."

"Magic?" Jimmy's eyes grew wide.

"Yes, Mr. Gold is quite the sleight of hand expert."

"Miss Maynard, would you care to join us?" Gold stood up and brushed off his pants. The linen was wrinkled, but he didn't seem to mind.

"Why, yes. That sounds nice." *See, Mother, I'm making the effort.*

Chapter 2

They made an odd group as they maneuvered through the two cars on the way to the dining car. Mr. Lewis was escorting her with a gentle hand in the cars and a firm assistance between the cars. He and Mr. Gold were handing Jimmy between themselves when they passed between cars. It was for safety, she was sure, but it made them feel like a family. She and Mrs. Wells as the wives. It was nice and a little strange all at once. It didn't seem right to be eating with two presumably single men.

"And do you have any children of your own, Mr. Gold?" Mrs. Wells asked.

"No." His smile was sad.

"You're very good with children."

"I had nieces and nephews to visit," he said with a shrug. "And I had six little brothers. My mother wanted a girl. After the seventh boy she abandoned the quest."

Mrs. Wells laughed softly at that. Iko let Mr. Lewis tuck her hand into the crook of his arm as they spoke to the waiter about a table for the five of them. The tables were set with maroon edged white cloths. Water and wine glasses glittered in the dappled sun. The silverware was polished to a reflective gleam. The waiter deftly removed the wine glass from Jimmy's spot. That was probably wise given the big eyes Jimmy had staring at the crystal. They ordered lunch.

She and Mrs. Wells sat with Jimmy between them on the bench. They ended up with the same arrangement as they'd had in the train. Iko was across from Mr. Lewis. Mrs. Wells was across from Mr. Gold. "And do you have children, Mr. Lewis?" Iko asked softly. She didn't want this conversation to carry too much. She didn't want the other people in the dining car to hear them. It was silly, but she didn't know them. Not even the little bit that she knew the people in her own car. She bit the inside of her lip to stay quiet and let Lewis answer.

"I did once," he stated. "I had a son."

Gold squeezed his shoulder and the conversation moved on quickly away from the topic. "Tell me, Miss Maynard, how did you decide to look for work in Boston?"

"My father suggested it. He'd made friends with a few men who are teachers there now. He thought it would be a good place for me to find a husband with a good future."

"And what is a good future? I could argue that I'd be an excellent husband." Gold winked at her.

"And everything would be lies," Mr. Lewis contradicted. "Never marry a man who can spin stories, Miss Maynard. It's simply not a safe line of work."

"I wouldn't marry a man who can't manage to wrinkle a newspaper, if I were you," Gold informed her. "It shows a lack of romantic gestures."

"If I had that newspaper in my hands right now, I'd be doing damage to your linen." Lewis' voice was lighter now. He looked out the window at the moving scenery. "It's so nice to be able to sit back and watch scenery flying by."

"As opposed to having to drive, stop for gas, meet people, have conversations, mingle with the people you don't spend time with. I like road trips. You get to see things that just blur by when you're on the train."

"Really? You like road trips so that you can meet people?" Iko's eyes widened. She hadn't thought of traveling like that. Traveling was to see places, not people.

"And find stories." Gold's smile showed off crooked front teeth and a small scar on his chin.

"You can find stories on a train. For instance, just today you've met Mrs. Wells and Miss Maynard, and Master James." Lewis said.

Their meals arrived and they nibbled on the roasted chicken and the cheese and crackers. Iko sipped at the wine that her companions insisted she try. It was sweet and bitter and the same time and had the strangest feeling of not being liquid in her tongue. It was white and tasted nothing like grape juice or the wine that they had at communion.

Mrs. Wells smiled at Mr. Gold as he described meeting a magician on one of his road trips. "I've managed to teach a few tricks to Lewis here, but he's just not the best student for me. Perhaps I can steal your son for the rest of the trip and teach him to produce coins from ears and noses."

"I think that would be a great use of his time. Thank you." Jimmy for his part was too concentrated on getting the food from his plate into his mouth without spilling it on his white sailor suit that he didn't even notice the suggestion that he would be learning magic on this trip. Iko absently wiped his mouth for him.

"Miss Maynard, you have siblings?"

"A brother," she confirmed. Mr. Lewis' eyes were solemn and his mouth had lost most of its smile during the discussion of teaching Jimmy tricks. With a pang she realized that he'd likely seen Gold teach his own son something like it. "He's turning sixteen in October."

"Will you be traveling back to Washington to visit him?"

She shook her head. "I'll send him a card. Possibly a camera. He's wanted one for ages."

"He wants to be a photographer?"

"For a newspaper. He wants to take pictures of famous people."

"He's still young, that may broaden," Lewis said.

"Will you be traveling to Boston?" She asked him. She rather hoped he would.

"No, I'll be getting off in New Jersey. I have proofs to pick up from a publisher there. I'm a copy editor."

"He's a nitpicker, in other words," Gold interjected.

"Oxford commas are your friends, Mr. Gold."

"Oxford commas are the bane of my existence, Mr. Lewis."

"I will not calm down. We keep missing stations!" That was Pam's voice ringing off the china and making the wine dance more than the vibration of the train. She was definitely a singer. "What if there's something wrong with the brakes?"

"Pam!" her companion's voice was sharp. "Stop it. Take a breath. Let's take a moment and smoke a cigarette, yeah?"

Lewis looked out the window. "There is something wrong out there." His voice was soft. "It's not the stations. Or rather not just the stations. The towns look empty."

"Maybe the stations are closed. The train simply doesn't stop there any longer. Or they've added a more direct route from DC to New York and we didn't notice?"

"I like that explanation," Mrs. Wells stated. "That's the one I'm going to believe for the moment. Perhaps you should give it to the young lady who keeps yelling out her fears."

"After lunch." Lewis nodded.

Chapter 3


"Mrs. Chattergee," the retired soldier said, "would you do me the honor of taking lunch with me?"

She smiled warmly at him. "Yes, General Clauson. Or would you rather I arrange to have something brought to you?"

"No, no. I should move." He got himself to his feet. He placed his cane down and leaned heavily against it. He waited for Mrs. Chattergee to join him. Her white cotton fabric swirled around her legs like clouds. She smiled kindly at Iko when she noticed she was watching. Her eyes showed her age when she did. A mother, Iko decided, with her children well grown. The general offered one of his walrus fins. She tucked a delicate hand into the crook of his arm. She helped him balance as they attempted to leave the car.

Lewis returned a moment later. Iko's nose wrinkled. She didn't like whatever tobacco he smoked. "I think Pam will be a bit calmer," he informed his companions. He winked at Gold. The action made Gold's brows raise.

"Seems to have calmed you a bit as well. You'll need to send your suit for cleaning."

"I seem to remember most jazz clubs smelling this way. She's an artist. Her," he paused. Iko could see him looking through the dictionary in his mind to find the right word. "Companion is a songwriter. He says his guitar is in the luggage room. We might be able to convince him to provide a bit of entertainment."

Gold chuckled. "But is he the right kind of music to be playing here?"

"I think he'll do. Never fear. He's got the right kind of mind to come up with rhymes on the spot. I had him in the midst of Shakespearian limericks by the end of our conversation. He also agreed that it might help ease Pam's paranoia."

"You think she's paranoid, or that there's a problem?" The two men glanced at the sleeping Jimmy before continuing. Mrs. Wells seemed to be reading her magazine as opposed to following the conversation.

"It's a problem. I haven't see cars moving on the main roads. And there seems to be abandoned towns all along this route. I can't understand it. There's usually at least a few children out to throw waves at or to shoot BB's at the side of the train. I haven't even glimpsed a hobo camp with a fire burning."

"It is a bit warm for a fire right now, don't you think?"

"Not to cook over. The whole idea of the places just being empty is eerie. I haven't seen a red light down the track either. There's no trains in the opposite direction. We should have passed at least a freight train by this point."

"Now, that you mention it, I haven't noticed one. Any sighting of the conductors?"

"No conductors. No porters. They might be at lunch in the back of the train in the colored car."

"Possible. Weren't there any porters up toward the front? Don't they stay with the first class passengers at all times?"

"The drapes were drawn on all the compartments, so I have no idea if they're full. I didn't make it to the very front of the train. I got sent back by the porter." He paused, frowning. "I think it was the first class porter. Maybe it was someone's bodyguard. It's all fuzzy."

Gold snorted. "I'm not surprised. Why don't you close your eyes for a quick nap and I'll turn my attention to teasing observations out of our letter writer when he returns from wherever he's hidden himself."

"Possibly the lavatory? I didn't pass him on the way back from the outside car."

"You saw General Walrus?"

"I did. And his lovely companion. Didn't you interview her once?"

"Mrs. Chattergee? I have no idea what you're talking about. I simply did a piece on the food of India. She helped me translate a few of the more esoteric spices into something that the American public would understand."

Staggering into the car a man in a wrinkled suit dropped heavily into the general's seat. "You guys have noticed that we're not on the right route right?" he pleaded. "I mean we were supposed to have four stops by now. And I'm heading home so I'm not going to be very happy if suddenly they've decided to change the route. Did you know about a route change?" His voice was slurred and he moved through his words as if they were pressing against the back of his throat and he couldn't do anything but let them free. He didn't pause long enough for any of them to answer him. "My ma will be angry if I don't get home in time for her birthday. You see the problem right?"

"Sir, calm down." Lewis spoke firmly.

"I'm calm. Why don't you think I'm calm?"

"Sir," Iko broke in. Perhaps it would make a difference. "We can't answer your questions if you're set on answering them yourself. Give us a minute to answer before you ask the next question."

His eyes fastened on her face. His expression transformed from worried to disgusted in a half a heartbeat. "Shut up, girl. I'm not going to take that kind of talk from a fucking Jap."

She winced back from his anger. Mrs. Wells put a steadying hand on her shoulder.

"Apologize to the lady," Lewis instructed.

"Fuck no."

"You, sir, are out of line. There are women present and you will not use that sort of language around them." Lewis stood. "Come, let's take a few steps back to your seat and we'll discuss things."

"Don't worry, Miss Maynard. He is drunk and drunks don't know how to hold their tongue." Gold leaned into the space between the banks of chairs. "He had no call to speak to you in those tones."

"But he did have cause to call me 'Jap'?" she challenged. "As if that's something wrong?"

Gold blinked at her. "My dear, be glad it was nothing more crude. At this point, that's all we can ask of a drunk, yes?"

She sighed. "Yes, I suppose. He could have called me much worse. Others have."

"Lewis will look after him. Hopefully, that will stop any more foolishness on his part."

"Leave me alone!"

"Sir, please calm down. There is no reason to be upset. Let's act like rational adults here," Lewis soothed.

"Oh, I can see he's handling it," Mrs. Wells said lifting her head. "I hope he handles him right out of the car."

"Maybe onto the tracks?" Gold offered with a sweet smile.

"Listen, fag, leave me alone."

"I need you to take a deep breath for me. Your heart seems to be beating very fast and it's making your face very red. It can't be good for you." Lewis kept his voice calm. He pressed a hand to the man's wrist.

"Get the fuck off of me."

"Sir."

The man roared and took a swing. Lewis dodged out of the way, only to be sprawled in the center of the aisle. He pushed himself to his feet rather than the crouch he'd been maintaining to talk to the man. "What's your name, sir?"

"You call me 'sir' or nothing. Get out of my face. I want to know what's going on here and I don't care who you have to find to tell me!"

"I don't work for the railroad."

"Touch me again and I'll lay you out. Fags, Japs, Wogs. Bet there's a kike on this train too."

Lewis' hands fisted. Iko watched him purposefully open them and force his shoulders down. The man must be really drunk to think that he'd have a chance to take someone else down. Iko hadn't seen a man this drunk since Miko's wedding. Her best friend had married well, but her father had hated the groom. He'd gotten drunk on the cheap wine that flowed too quickly at the reception and tried to take a swing at Miko's new husband. "You just sit here and stay quiet and we'll find someone to take care of you."

Lewis' voice was calm and cheerful. He returned to his seat. "I hope he gets up and tries to leave the car."

"Tries? You think he's stable enough for that?"

"Possibly."

"He is right. There is something going on. I for one wouldn't mind if we get a real answer from the railroad. I'll try getting through first-class." Gold got up. He checked his pocket for something. "Might I borrow your pen?"

Lewis handed up a gold pen. "If you lose that, I'll take it out of your hide."

"I apologize for his deplorable habits, ladies. If you'll excuse me."

Lewis ran a hand through his hair, then, borrowed Gold's hat from the seat. "I think Jimmy has the right idea. If you'll pardon me. I'm going to close my eyes for a few minutes. Maybe I'll be able to come up with a rational explanation."

The drunk continued to splutter, but he was fading. He slipped into a dazed sleep. Iko covered a yawn with her hand. What on earth was happening? The train wasn't that comfortable. She looked around. Most people had dozed off. Pam was sleeping in the corner of her chair. She seemed smaller now. Younger and older at the same time. Iko pushed herself up from the seat with some difficulty. She waited until she felt steady before making her way to the lavatory.

She opened it and stepped in. Her nose wrinkled immediately at the smell. The floor was linoleum in a strange meld of beiges. She hung her purse on the provided hook and tucked her gloves inside of it. While she was washing her hands, her glance caught the mirror. There was another set of eyes there. She spun and found the room empty. Her heart beat like bird's. She swallowed hard and wiped her hands on the towel.

She wobbled on her way back to her seat. The drunk man caught her wrist. "Sit with me."

"No." She tugged against his grip. Her eyes darted through the car, looking for rescue. Pam's lover was watching with avid eyes, but he didn't seem inclined to help.

"Sit with me," he repeated. "I'll pay your usual rates, just sit with me."

"Let me go," she said firmly. "I can't sit down, the seats are all taken."

"Sit on my lap."

She twisted in his grip, feeling the bones in her wrist grinding. "Let go of me." Her voice rose.

"What's the matter? My money not good enough for you? Damned whores are all alike."

She couldn't stop herself. It was as if her body were under someone else's control. She slapped him hard across the face. The sound echoed like a shot around the car. He stared at her, his eyes clearer suddenly. He nearly threw her hand back to her. He looked at her with wide eyes. He lurched up from his seat to the lavatory. The door didn't close quickly enough to disguise the sound of his retching. She tottered back to her seat and collapsed. She rubbed at her wrist. She pulled her gloves back on. Her fingers trembled.

"Are you okay?" the songwriter asked. His voice was low, but it carried.

She nodded somewhat jerkily.

He looked down at his sleeping sweetheart. "People try the same thing with her. All the time. I'm Ben."

"Iko."

Chapter 4

Gold was unsteady and pale when he returned. He shook Lewis roughly on the shoulder. The man didn't rouse. A few light smacks to the cheek did nothing either. "If you don't wake up, I'll kiss you." Gold stood up straight. "Huh. That almost always works. He must really be asleep."

Iko simply looked at him. She was still rubbing her wrist. Her tormentor hadn't returned from the lavatory. She hoped he'd drowned. "Do you threaten him with kissing often?"

Gold chuckled. "I used to threaten to lick him, but after he had a child and a dog, that didn't work quite so well. It used to make his wife laugh. I suppose it might have been her laughter that woke him more than the kiss though."

"Does wine usually make him sleep so deeply?"

"No. Not unless he's take a sleep aid with it." He glanced at the songwriter. "Did he perchance borrow your cigarette earlier?"

Ben quirked a grin at him. He nodded.

"Nothing to do for it then." Gold grabbed Lewis by the front of his jacket and pulled him from the seat and dumped him to the floor. Lewis yelped as he hit the ground.

"I should have drowned you when we were children."

"Up you get now." Gold manhandled him back into his seat. Lewis rubbed his eyes like a tired child. Iko hid her laughter. Cousins, she finally decided. They'd known each other for years and years, yet weren't actually brothers. Her wrist didn't hurt quite so much anymore. "Can you focus for me? There's no one in first class."

"What?"

"No one. None of the compartments are filled."

"That's implausible. First class dining car?" Lewis' eyes seemed to focus more sharply now.

"Empty."

"Luggage?"

"No luggage. No porter. There are tickets on the compartments. They indicate stops we've passed by. I don't know what that means. Just that they seem to have gotten off while we haven't even paused," Gold said.

"We need to find the conductor who was dealing with our tickets. Whatever happened to the man who was in the far corner?"

"You double check the front, I'll start heading back. See if anyone's noticed him. Perhaps he's simply getting drunk in the dining car," Gold suggested.

The general and Mrs. Chattergee reappeared. He didn't look particularly well. His face was wan and his arm was trembling under her hand. He was leaning heavily on the dog-headed cane. She settled him and looked up in worry at the others in the car. "We were in the dining car when one of the men disappeared."

"What?"

"One of the businessmen at the table next to us disappeared. As if he'd never been there. He trembled and shuttered like a melting piece of motion picture film and then disappeared." Her voice was softly accented, similar to the general's but different enough that you could tell she wasn't English. She settled back in her seat across from the general. "We both saw it, yet his companions didn't seem to notice. It was as if he'd never been there. His plate was still there and his wine only half-full. We were put off our feed and came back directly."

"I think that may have been what happened to our man in the corner. Where's our drunk friend?" Lewis asked.

"Having a wretched time in the bathroom," Ben smirked. "I say leave the bastard to it."

"Language, dear," Pam said fuzzily. "We're around squares."

"Go back to sleep, lovely."

She hummed her agreement. If she found out about flickering people, Iko thought she might panic even more. That wouldn't do any of them any good. "Isn't there supposed to be a tea cart coming around?"

"At four," Lewis stated. "We can see if it shows up or not. And question the server. Good thought."

Iko smiled at that. "Are you still going exploring?"

The general coughed. "My dear, I think it would be best if you were to stay here." He seemed to have thought she were going with Lewis.

She blinked. "General, there is no reason to think this car is any safer than the rest of this train."

"Perhaps not, but it we do seem to be able to think in this car."

"Where has our letter writer gone. Did anyone see him in the dining car?" Lewis asked.

"No. Not in first class either," Gold answered. He glanced over at the seat and the neatly labeled letters. They were addressed and sealed. Iko stood up. She reached up to tug on the ticket that indicated his stop. She was too short. "Let me, Miss Maynard." Lewis pulled it off and looked at it. "Newark. We haven't passed Newark yet."

"Which means, if this is following logic, he should still be on the train? Is it possible he was investigating as well?" Iko pressed.

"There is nothing inherently logical about people disappearing from a train," Lewis pointed out. His face was solemn, but his eyes were crinkling in humor.

"Stop baiting her. She's making a good point. He should still be here. The first class evidence does point to this being related to the stops that we're passing by," Gold chided.

"Sorry." Lewis looked away from them. He reached over for the letters and the papers there. His hand passed through them. He blinked and tried again. "Dom, am I drunk?"

"Not that drunk." Gold reached for the top letter. His fingers passed through them as well.

Iko felt light-headed. She sat down heavily on her seat. "Mrs. Wells?" She touched her arm. "Jimmy?" She reached across Mrs. Well's lap to shake him. The little boy shouldn't be that deeply asleep. Gold reached over immediately to check Mrs. Wells pulse.

"Mrs. Chattergee? I don't know that you remember me, but I'm Dom Gold. You worked with me on an article on Indian spices that were new to the United States?"

"You are unforgettable, Mr. Gold," she replied with a serene smile. "What is it you need?"

"I recall that you were trained as a nurse? Could you check our friends here?"

"Of course." She stepped across the aisle and crowded into the space between Iko's knees and Gold's body. She seemed unconcerned by the closeness of the quarters. She checked Mrs. Wells' breathing, her pupils, and her pulse. She did the same for Jimmy. She frowned. "As far as I can determine, they are simply asleep. There seems to be no evidence of drugs or concussion. They should awaken."

"Can you check the others? We know that Pam's roused a bit and our drunk is possibly passed out in the lavatory, but the others should have awakened at least a bit when we started talking."

She nodded. "Come with me, Miss Maynard. I think it best you learn this."

Iko blinked. "Yes, ma'am." She'd never turned her nose up at knowledge.

"Here, press your first two fingers here. You should feel a rhythmic pressure against your fingertips. Do you feel it?" At Iko's nod, Mrs. Chattergee held up a silver watch. "Start counting now. And stop." The lessons continued until the older woman was satisfied that she'd be able to do it on her own.

"Your stop is before Boston," Iko said quietly.

"It is. Much like Mr. Lewis'. You may need to do this without me. If there's any choice involved, I shall stay." Her hands were rough with the callouses of someone who'd done physical work for most of her life. "Do not be afraid, Miss Maynard."

Iko looked at the older woman for a long moment. "I am afraid."

"Then have courage. Things always seem darker than they are."

Gold and Ben had wrestled the drunk back into a seat in the section opposite of Pam and Ben's. "God," the man breathed. He rubbed at his temples. "What is wrong with you people?"

"We're sober," Gold said. He was frowning. "You strike me as the sort of man who doesn't drink wine."

"I don't. Pansies drink wine." He looked Gold up and down. "As I'm sure you know."

Lewis sat very still, but the way his jaw was clenched told Iko he really wanted to jump into the conversation. She took her seat after sending a glare in their drunk's direction. Clauson, the old general, stood up. His face had regained its normal coloring. He loomed over the man. "On your feet, soldier," he snapped.

The drunk gulped and jumped to his feet with a salute. He wavered on his feet a bit.

"Name and rank."

"Lt. Paul Serendinski, US Navy, sir."

"Drunk sailor." He snorted. "Not unusual. Now, Lt., if you're not going to be helpful, we'll pack you into the luggage room and make you watch your mouth. Do you understand me?"

The younger man winced. "Yes, sir."

"Sit down and answer the questions with a civil tongue and I won't have to make you clean the head with your tie."

"Yes, sir." Serendinski sat with his head in his hands. "You had questions?"

"We're trying to sort out what's happening on this train. Did you drink the white wine in the dining car?" Gold began again.

"No. I had a gin and tonic."

"Just a gin and tonic."

The sailor barked out a laugh. "No. Not just one. I never stop at one."

"Which entree did you try?"

"I had the chicken. It was the only thing I recognized as actual food."

Iko bit her lip and looked down at her lap. That's the same thing she'd thought when she looked at the menu. She pressed a fingernail into the side of Mrs. Wells' wrist. She didn't react. She didn't even pull away in reflex. She opened her mouth, but then glanced at Lewis. He shook his head. She let the questions go. He wouldn't answer her. "You didn't have the chicken." She kept her voice low.

"No, but I did have, um, other substances between lunch and sleeping. It's possible that that might have mitigated or changed the nature of the items."

"Or it has to do with something that's internal to us rather than an outside source."

"But attempting to figure out what all of us have in common will take far too long. I have to wonder what we think we're doing here. Are we trying to stop it, or just determine what's causing it?" The look in his eyes made Iko freeze. His eyes were shining as if he were about to cry.

"We're trying to stop it, of course," Iko said.

"Why?" Lewis asked. Iko felt herself go very still.

"What?"

"Why are we trying to stop it? We have no evidence that it's a bad thing. In fact, we have no evidence that this isn't some bizarre dream."

"Sam, quiet." Gold's voice was calm. He dropped a hand onto Lewis' shoulder without looking away from his interrogation of Mr. Serendinski.

"Don't quiet me, Dom. It's something we need to think about. Do we think it's bad simply because it's unusual? Or do we actually feel threatened by it? Do we feel as though something horrible is happening to these people or are they just leaving us?"

Iko glanced over at Mrs. Chattergee. She was smiling her serene smile. She and the General were discussing something in a language Iko couldn't identify.

"Sam, please, don't get into this again." Gold squeezed the hand on Lewis' shoulder. "It wasn't your fault. You didn't do anything wrong. Don't let it color this for you."

"Really, Dom? Are you so sure I couldn't have done anything to save them because I'm not. I just. I just think we need to decide what we think we're doing."

"Sam, look at me." Gold broke away from his conversation to squat down so he and  Lewis were looking each other in the eyes. "I really need you with me right now. I need you focused on solving this. Bring those sharp eyes and all the information you have hiding in your head to bear on the subject. Don't get caught up in your guilt and pain. I know that a nip of pot does this to you. It always has. I can't stop you from feeling this way, but I need you to focus. For me, please."

Lewis closed his eyes. He nodded. "I'll start... start writing down what we know. We can pass the paper around and write down what we ate for lunch. That sort of thing."

"Good man."

Lewis' head started to nod. Gold shook him awake before he could fall all the way. Ben was rousing Pam to full wakefulness now. "Let me sleep," she murmured. "God. Just let me sleep. I'm so tired."

"I can't do that, sweetheart. Wake up. Stay with me now. I need you."

Pam sat up. She rubbed her eyes, smearing her mascara and making her look as if she'd been crying. She sheepishly pulled a handkerchief out of her purse and wiped at her face and hands. "Where's the guy who was in the seat across from me?"

"We don't know. I didn't see him get up."

"I was drawing him earlier." She pulled out her sketchbook and flipped to the page. She stared at it. "This isn't right. This isn't what he looked like at all."

Chapter 5

Pam shook her head as Ben tried to flip through her book. "I know who I've drawn. This isn't the man I was drawing. I'm telling you that he looked nothing like this. This looks more like Mr. Lewis over there or even the drunk sailor. This looks nothing like the businessman who was sitting right there." She pointed at the seat with two fingers. Her charcoal was gripped between her fingers now.

"Maybe it's on a different sheet of paper. I think you should let me look through and see if there's something here that you don't recognize." Ben slid his hand up her arm to settle on her wrist. There was something loving and possessive both in the movement. It was nothing that Iko had seen before. Not in person. They touched constantly, but she didn't wear a ring. She didn't wear any jewelry. No hat, no gloves, nothing so simple as a matching purse. Her purse was oversized, and more like a schoolbag than a purse.

"Stop it. I'm not that high. I didn't drink any of the wine. Everyone else here did." She scowled. "Well most of you had alcohol. Maybe that's what did this. We're all just on a really bad high and when we wake up will just be on the train toward Boston and not stuck in the middle of something strange like this." She also didn't talk like anyone Iko had ever met.

"I wish I believed that. I really do," Ben said quietly.

"I wish you believed it too." She buried her face in Ben's shoulder. "I'm tired. I just want to go to sleep. Why is it a bad thing to sleep?"

"Because the people who fall asleep here aren't waking up. Even the kid's not waking up and we all know that he should be awake right now."

"I don't know. He looks comfortable. Fine. Where's the coffee cart? If we need to stay awake, I'm going to need some help."

"May I look at your work?" Iko asked. She crossed the aisle to settle in the seat of the missing businessman. Never let anyone say she couldn't read a situation. Lewis needed to be alone for a minute. She didn't know the full story, but Gold needed to talk him down. They needed his help if they were going to get out of this. She knew that somewhere deep in her chest. But Pam was important too. She could see something that the rest of them couldn't. And talking about her work might help her stay awake.

"You might want to take off your gloves. There's probably charcoal on the pages."

Iko nodded. She tucked her gloves into the small purse. It looked like a darling thing next to the pouch that Pam carried. She looked at the drawings. "Who is this?"

"That's the conductor that we met in New Orleans when we got onto the train. We've been traveling for days now." She smiled. "Can't afford one of the compartments. Why would we want to anyway? You can't meet new people when you lock yourself up in a room."

She turned to a picture of a dancer. "And this?"

"That's Liza. She's in Atlanta now. She's trying out for the ballet company." Pam's smile was fond. "She's a lovely woman."

Page by page Pam gave small histories of the people she'd drawn. "And who is this?"

"That's the businessman who was sitting in your seat. He's going home to visit his son who lives in Philadelphia." She froze. "Oh my God. How did I forget that? How could I look at that picture and not know him."

"Will you draw someone for me?"

"Who?"

"Anyone. I want to know how you see them."

She cocked her head to the side. "Okay. Will you put your gloves back on for me?"

Iko blinked. "Why yes, of course." She sat with her hands neatly in her lap. Ben looked at her with amusement.

"Tell me, Iko, why are you on this train?"

"I'm heading to Boston. I'll be working at the college."

"And your father is the one who got you the job."

"Yes. He thinks I'll find a husband."

"And is a husband what you want." Ben lifted his brows. His eyes were green she noticed. His hair was shaggy like a sheepdog. His beard was long and bushy even though it was groomed. He looked like someone who'd drive her parents to distraction. He was more of a rebel than the young man she'd dated in high school. That boy had gone on to join the Navy.

"I don't know. Perhaps I'll fall madly in love with a professor."

Pam glanced up with a smile. "Maybe you'll fall madly in love with an artist."

"Or an engineer," Iko shot back.

"A poet."

"Heaven forbid. A day laborer."

"A Negro?" Pam raised her brows.

Iko shook her head. "It will be hard enough to convince a white man's mother to let me marry him."

Ben chuckled. "It's not as hard as you might think. Just let her know that she won't have to feed him or get his clothes in wearable condition and that you love him."

Pam snorted. "Which is why I won't be marrying this man." She gestured with her charcoal. "There's no way to make those clothes more acceptable to his mother."

Iko laughed at that.

"There you are." Pam grinned. "I had wondered if there was a real girl hiding inside of the china doll."

"I'm not a doll."

"You're perfect. A cherry blossom doll." Pam turned the drawing to face her. Iko put a hand to her mouth. Pam had drawn her surrounded by cherry blossoms. Her eyes were dark and older than they ought to be. She was wearing the hints of a formal kimono, but the drawing stopped at her shoulders. Her dark hair, currently pulled back into a simple braid was curled into sleek lines and coiled around a long slender pin.

"What's this?"

"An Arizona toothpick. A stiletto, in any other state."

Iko touched the charcoal, heedless of the black transferring to her white gloves. "Draw Mr. Lewis for me, please."

Pam raised her brows. "A crush?"

Iko ducked her head. "No. Just an idea."

Pam crossed the room and settled into Iko's seat. Gold was back to his interrogation. He'd drawn out as much as Iko thought he'd be able to get. He kept going though. She didn't know what he was looking for now. Ben cocked his head. "You think Pam's seeing something because of the drugs?"

"I don't know. She and Mr. Lewis are the only two who are somewhere between awake and asleep. It might mean something. Maybe they have something in common that we don't know."

"Beyond a toke, I don't know what. Look at them. He's a corporate dandy. She's a beat girl. It's like saying you and she have something in common beyond being women."

"I don't know. You don't know me well enough to determine that."

"No. I know her though. She's my everything. No matter how many time people try to tell me she's nothing but a whore or ignore her writing or her pictures. They're fools. She's the most incredible thing that's ever happened to me." Ben's eyes were soft as they focussed on his lover.

"If you love her, why haven't you married her?"

"Marriage is nothing but another way for the state to control us. They tell us how we're allowed to like each other, how we live together. They want her to lose her name become part of me instead of being herself. I don't want a Mrs. I want my Pam."

"What's her last name?"

"Rook. Pamela Rook." Ben's smile exposed surprising white, straight teeth.

"And you?"

"Ben Harmon." He winked. "Maybe you'll hear about us in a newspaper some day."

Pam and Lewis were in a conversation now. Ben glanced over at them. "You wanted her to pull him out of it. Out of whatever has him so quiet right now. There's something really interesting about him. Pam's never that intent if there's not something interesting."

"He's a good person. He and Gold have known each other since childhood."

Ben raised his brows. "Did they. Still, I noticed something was going on with the seat over there?"

"Oh, the letters. None of us can touch them, but they're still sitting there."

"What the..." Lewis' voice cut through the air. Everyone turned. Iko was up and across the aisle to see. She peeked over Pam's head. The letters were gone.

"Did they fade out or just disappear?" Iko asked.

"They flickered and then they were gone. We haven't reached Newark have we?"

"No, but all of first class' luggage is gone." Gold frowned. "I think we need to see if there's anyone else awake on this train."

"Coffee? Tea?" The cart pushed its nose through the door with the help of a black man in a starched white uniform. He offered once more and his eyes widened in surprise as he was surrounded by passengers asking for both.

"Are there many people on the train today?"

"Not buying coffee. Everyone's decided to take a nap. Looks like it hit in here too."

"We haven't seen a conductor in hours." Clauson made the statement seem like a complaint. It was an impressive twist of his tone. Iko took her tea and settled back into the seat across from Ben. She didn't want to break whatever connection Lewis and Pam had created.

The man laughed. "Probably down getting something to eat. I'll send one up when I see one."

"Thank you."

Gold took a coffee for himself and handed one to Lewis without asking. "Pam?"

"Black tea, please."

"So, Mr....?" Gold let the sentence trail off with raised brows.

"Norris. Thank you, sir." The cart man gave Gold a friendly smile as he poured Pam's tea.

"Everyone's asleep. Is there anyone still in the dining car?"

"No, the staff chases everyone out when it's closed down."

"Is the train as full as usual?"

Norris thought for a moment. "Now that you mention it, sir, it's a bit more full than usual. But with most of the customers asleep it's not so big of a difference to my cart." He shrugged. His crisp white jacket moved seemly on its own due to the starch. Pam received her tea with a smile. "Anything else I can get for you?"

"That's all. Thank you, Mr. Norris." Gold let the man pass with a smile. He waited until the door to first class closed behind him, then darted forward. He managed to pull the door open and not spill his coffee. He stood frozen in the doorway.

"Gold?" Lewis was on his feet, his coffee abandoned on Gold's seat.

"It's gone, Sam."

"What's gone?"

"First class. All of the cars. And Norris too."

Gold stumbled back to his chair. Pam grabbed her tea quickly before he could sit on it. He collapsed, hands shaking. "We're all still here. It's okay." He took the time to keep his voice steady.

"You could have been there, double-checking." Lewis gulped down his coffee. He looked as if he could have done with something a bit stronger.

"But I wasn't. There's no way of knowing if it would have disappeared if I'd been there."

Pam crossed to return to her seat. She sat there, knees up. Her fingers were stained with black now and there were smudges on the cuffs of her shirt. Iko glanced down and saw the faint traces of charcoal on her own dress. She frowned at them.

"May I see your drawing?"

Pam handed the sketchpad over. The face that looked up from it was a few years older than the Lewis Iko recognized. His hair was cut painfully short and he was wearing glasses. His tie was just as tightly tied and the tie-bar was still in place. His expression was bland. As if he felt nothing at all. His eyes though, his eyes were hard to look at. She couldn't explain it, but she saw pain and a suggestion of fire there. Around him was the suggestion of pages and pages of dense script. His face was framed with the simple lines.

"And Mr. Gold?"

Pam raised her brows. "Can't have one without the other, I suppose. How's your wrist?"

"Oh, it's fine."

"It's bruised."

"Mr. Serendinski grabbed me."

"Ben told me. You slapped him too?"

"He deserved it."

"Yes, he did. He had no right. No right to grab you. No right to call you names. You have the right to do whatever you want with your body." Pam's eyes were clear. The things she said though. Those made Iko's heart beat faster. Pam reached out a hand. She moved slowly and Iko let her peel down the top of her glove to expose the blue ring of bruises. She traced them with a smudged fingertip. Iko shivered. The bruises didn't hurt. The touch didn't hurt. But it surprised her. Pam gave her a sad smile. "Don't let anyone hurt you like that Iko."

The artist turned her attention to her drawing. Iko's mother would hate Pam. She would hate the suggestion that Iko be anything but the good and quiet girl she'd raised. Serendinski was no different than the soldiers that had guarded the internment camps. Her mother'd been grabbed and shoved and never raised a hand against them. Iko had already broken the silent promise to her mother that she'd be as forgiving once. She wasn't going to do it again. Words shouldn't hurt her.

Gold had regained his composure and was sipping at his coffee. He was listing toward Lewis' seat, but that was to be expected. Lewis seemed more alert now that he had someone to look after. Maybe that was all they needed, to take care of each other.

Serendinski was looking at Iko with narrowed eyes. Her heart clenched. "What?" she asked him. Her mother's voice was screaming in the back of her mind. Don't be rude! Be nice, be kind, be silent. Don't question him.

"You look just like a geisha I knew in Okinawa." He didn't say anything more than that, but she drew away as far as she could without leaving her seat. She desperately wanted to see what Pam made of Gold. Then, she'd ask her to draw the drunk. She needed to know why he frightened her more than the idea of people disappearing out of their seats, of letters flickering away like illusions, or of entire train cars vanishing with the opening of a door.

Mrs. Chattergee let out a startled "Oh."

"Ma'am?" Lewis asked, standing to cross over to her.

"The woman who was next to me disappeared. Her seat is completely empty. It startled me." She seemed calm enough, but Iko went to sit by her anyway. Lewis took Iko's seat. Possibly to continue whatever conversation he'd been having with Pam. "I am well, Miss Maynard."

Iko took her hand. The older woman gave her a tired smile. "You didn't notice until she was gone?"

"I was listening to General Clauson's story. When I turned my head back she was no longer there. There was no sound."

"Seat check," Gold stated. "Who else has missing seatmates?"

Iko stood to count sleeping heads in the aisle seating areas closest to the First class doors. "Two gone on the left side. One on the right."

"Four gone here." Serendinski's voice was tight. "Fuck. I was looking right at one. Flickered out of existence."

"What do you think would happen if we moved them?" Ben asked. "Put all the sleepers in one place?"

There was quiet in the car. "I don't know, son," the general said finally. "Don't know if it's worth the risk."

"We might be able to wake some of them up." Gold was excited. "I got Lewis to wake up."

Iko stood uncertainly in the aisle. She wasn't sure if she wanted to try waking up Mrs. Wells. It might break her heart if it didn't work. Gold didn't have the same problem. He was across the aisle trying to wake Mrs. Wells a moment later. It was as if he couldn't stand the thought of her asleep for one more moment. He shook her roughly. He looked as if he wanted to try dropping her to the floor as he had Lewis, but he couldn't bring himself to truly lay hands on her.

Pam had no such compunctions. She grabbed the man in the seat across from her by the lapels and pulled him off of his seat. He hit the floor in a boneless sprawl. He let out a snuffling snore, but didn't rouse. "Somehow, I don't think it's going to be that easy, Mr. Gold," she said. She kissed the businessman in the next seat. That didn't do anything. He didn't even twitch away from her touch or turn toward it. She held him closely for a moment to be sure.

Serendinski looked shocked at her actions. His jaw was dropped open and his eyes were wide. He stared at

Pam as if he hadn't noticed her before. Pam pinched and slapped the last man in their area. That also led to no reaction. "I don't think they're just asleep. I think they're in a coma or something," she said reasonably.

"They did not exhibit any of the symptoms of true coma. Except, of course, for not waking. Even coma patients will have some reflex reactions unless they are truly dead. They will move from pain. They will react. Some will even spontaneously open their eyes without waking." Mrs. Chattergee's voice was calm and even.

"So asleep by some sedative?"

"They do not have the enlarged pupils I would expect from someone who was drugged." The Indian woman shrugged her shoulders. "It is possible that it is some new drug that I have not been trained to recognize."

"Or it could just be magic or something supernatural. At this point, I am willing to entertain any explanation." Lewis' voice was surprisingly even. There was a tightness around his eyes, however, that made him seem less than calm. "We need to see if there's still a car behind us. Ben, can you put this gentleman back into his seat on your own or do you need a hand?"

"I'll help him," Serendinski said. "Wouldn't mind tossing someone around right now."

"I'll check the back door." Gold moved to open the door on the opposite side of the car from first class.

"Looks as if the other cars are still there. Well, I can't tell how many of them, that is, but the one that was there a few minutes ago is still there."

"Don't step out without me."

"Wouldn't dream of it." The linen clad man looked over his shoulder with an oddly fond expression. "If only you'd say that on a Saturday night maybe you wouldn't be so lonely."

"Oh, shut up. I haven't found anyone to replace my wife. That is not a crime in this world."

"You having no one to play with is certainly a crime. You need to be entertained or else you become as dour as a monk who won't drink the ceremonial wine."

"Are you quite finished, Gold?"

"I am never finished when it comes to teasing you."

Lewis swallowed the last of his coffee. "We're off. We'll be back in twenty minutes by my watch. If we're not back, best of luck. And it wasn't a choice, for whatever the knowledge is worth to you."

Iko nodded. The general stood. "No, lads. You're younger than I am. They'll need you more than they need me. I'll do the recon. You look after the ladies." He planted his cane firmly in the plush carpet. He stalked toward the doors. The two men gave way before him. He patted Lewis on the shoulder. "Keep your head, son." He nodded to Gold. "Gather everything we know together on paper. We'll review it when I get back." He checked his watch. "Twenty minutes."

"Twenty minutes," Gold confirmed, looking at his silver pocket-watch. He set it back into his pocket as the door closed behind the general. "I do not like the idea of him out there alone."

"I don't like the idea of him not coming back more," Pam stated. Iko crossed to sit in the open seat next to Pam. She stepped over the sleeping man that Ben and Serendinski were considering as one would consider a load of wood.

"Let's drag him over to the back corner, since he's not waking up anyway. We can call it an experiment," Ben said.

Serendinski snorted. "I've got the left arm."

"You want to see Mr. Gold?" Pam held the sketchpad out for her. Iko took it, her white gloves were irreparably stained already. She stared at the picture of a much younger man. He was no more than seventeen.

"This is Mr. Gold?" She stared at the picture. This was not what she saw when she looked at him. "He seems so much older to me."

"Does he? He looks like a kid. He's younger than Bill. I guessed that he was Mr. Lewis' teenager or something."

"No, he's the same age as Mr. Lewis. At least that's what I assumed." She kept her voice low. This was something that she didn't want to share with the men yet. There was something here beyond Pam's ability to draw. There was something she didn't quite understand.

"Do you want me to do Serendinski?"

"And Mrs. Chattergee if you can. I think it's important. You see something that I don't. Something that I can only hint at."

"You need to try weed." Pam gave her a weak smile. "I'll take a look at Mrs. C first. I think the fabric will be interesting to draw. And you can go pester Mr. Lewis to let you take down some short hand to get into practice."

"I do not have a crush on Mr. Lewis." Iko glared at the other woman.

Pam was unrepentant. She winked. "That's okay. You don't have to like him to sleep with him, you now."

Iko blushed at that. "You are awful."

"I know. But if you like, I could sleep with you instead?" Pam batted her lashes.

"Stop that." Iko swatted her on the head with the sketchbook. "I think you need to just draw."

Pam took the book back. "As you command." She strode purposefully over to Mr. Lewis first though. "Let Iko take it down in shorthand. She needs the practice. She's going to be a secretary, you know."

"Odd, I thought she was going to be an administrator."

"There's nothing to say they won't let her be both, but she's going to need to practice in any case."

"Good idea. Miss Maynard? Would you be so kind as to take down the information as we organize it?"

Iko sent a narrow-eyed glare at Pam. "Of course, Mr. Lewis. Do you have paper and a pen? I didn't bring a stenopad with me."

"I have some." Gold handed over his pad of paper and Mr. Lewis' gold pen. She smiled.

"Thank you." She settled back into her seat. Jimmy and Mrs. Wells seemed to be sleeping peacefully.

"What we know for sure is that people are disappearing. First class was empty when we first investigated it. It didn't have people or luggage. The car is now completely missing. Our car is directly connected to the luggage car. We have no real idea of the criteria for the missing people. It doesn't seem to be connected to the tickets they've purchased. The first class compartments were all tagged with stations which we had passed by. The people who were here didn't actually disappear with their stations. At least Letters didn't."

"But that doesn't mean he hadn't planned to get off earlier and let everyone think he'd carried on to Newark," Gold interjected. "This could have something to do with the actual plans as opposed to whatever is on the tickets. Could we will ourselves off of the train?"

"But we don't know what happens when we do that. There's no guarantee that it's going to be any better off of the train. Let's not experiment with that particular thought." Lewis' shoulders hunched.

"We don't know how to wake the people who are on the train with us still. We think that they need to be awakened though, or else they'll disappear."

"And we don't know if there still is staff. Mr. Norris disappeared along with first class as far as we know." Lewis tapped his fingers on the arm of his seat.

"Gen. Clauson and Mrs. Chattergee were the first to actually witness a disappearance. And they were the only two in the car who found it to be distressing or out of the ordinary. The staff didn't react to it. Nor did the eating companions the man was with. So that implies that we have some sort of information or perspective that the average person on this train lacks." Gold crossed his ankles and stole his hat back to play with the brim.

"We still don't know what all of the people who are awake in this car have in common. We didn't all eat the same foods at lunch and we aren't all headed to the same destinations. I, for one, would like this resolved before the Newark Station."

Gold gripped Lewis' arm tightly. "I'd rather not watch you flicker out of existence like a melting piece of film."

"We don't know that will happen if I'm awake."

"It happened to the man in the dining car."

"True. We can't seem to rouse people who did eat the same meal. And we know for a fact that little Jimmy didn't have any wine or anything else that should be keeping him asleep like this. Maybe there's something in the air that we're immune to? Something like a sleeping gas or a virus that only puts us to sleep? Pam and I had mild cases of it? Some new experimental weapon?"

"That's possible, but I've never heard of something like that in the States." The door of the car opened and everyone turned to see the general return.

Chapter 6

The general stumped into the car and back to his seat. He collapsed there with a hearty expelling of breath. He closed his eyes for a moment. Iko wanted to get up and hover over him until he told her everything. There was no polite way to do that though, so she didn't move from where she was taking notes. She simply moved to a new page and titled it "The General's Exploration".

"I found only one other person awake. The staff is not available. I wasn't able to make it all the way to the back cars. I wouldn't have made it back in time. I'm not as quick as I used to be." He huffed out a laugh. "I've no idea if the luggage or freight cars have been affected or if they even exist. I saw no evidence of porters. There was no evidence of weapons or violence in any of the cars. The passengers are simply asleep."

"The other person who was awake?" Gold's voice was soft.

"Was a child. She would not leave her mother with a strange man and I found that to be very wise. However, if young Miss Maynard were to go talk to her, perhaps she could be convinced to join us here."

"I have cards for her to play with," Gold offered.

"There's also some colored crayons in my satchel," Pam offered from where she was seated on the floor drawing the hem and folds of Mrs. Chattergee's outfit. "And I have an extra sketchbook. She could draw or color if she liked."

"Thank you, Miss Pam." The general gave her a paternal smile.

"I'll go." Iko stood. "Where is she?"

"The third car back. Where the non-existent dining car once was."

Iko huffed out a breath of her own. It wasn't a laugh, but it was as close as she was able to produce.

"I'll walk with you," Ben stated.

"I think I should be able to make it there and back on my own. We don't want to worry her with a strange man."

"I'll smoke a cigarette in between the cars so that I can keep an eye on you and on the other cars. Is that okay?"

Iko glanced at Pam. The artist nodded in encouragement. "Thank you, Ben."

He gave her a shy smile. "I can be a gentleman. Sometimes. She'll probably be more upset by my beard. Most kids are. They haven't seen a beard that wasn't on their grandfather."

Iko smiled at that. "And yours is a most impressive beard."

"It is. I've worked very hard on it." The first step between the cars was a bit nerve-wracking. Iko held onto the side of the wall, the handle there was smooth and slippery under her gloves. She considered taking the gloves off and putting them into her purse, but that seemed to be too much trouble. Besides, she would be more comforting if she were properly dressed; like a lady with her hat and gloves and purse all matching.

She smoothed down the crumpled edge of her skirt as she paused just inside the next car. She checked the passengers as they moved by. There were many empty seats now. She counted no more than six people in each car they passed through. Then, in the third car, there was only one couple and their daughter. The little girl was maybe seven. Her hair was plaited into two braids with little blue bows at the bottom that matched her simple blue sundress. She had shiny black shoes on. She looked up with bright blue eyes.

"Hello. My name is Miss Maynard." Iko crouched down to meet her eyes. She could smell the tobacco of Ben's cigarette where it drifted through the door. It smelled like the ones her mother snuck behind the house because she still thought it was uncouth for a woman to smoke.

"I'm Nora."

"Nora, it must be rather boring to be here while your parents are asleep."

The little girl bit her lip. "It is a bit. I have my book though, so I'll be okay."

"Would you like to come with me to my car? There's a young lady there who says she has some crayons and paper you can use. And we have cards for playing Go Fish or Old Maid."

Nora cocked her head to the side. "I suppose. But Mother will be upset if she wakes up and I'm not here."

"Let me write her a note. Would that be okay?"

Nora's face cleared. "Yes, that would be okay. Thank you."

Iko found a discarded ticket stub and wrote on it with Mr. Lewis' pretty gold pen. She left it sitting in the middle of Nora's seat. She offered her hand to the young girl. They walked down the aisle. "Have you seen anything interesting on your trip so far?"

"I saw people disappear like in a magic show." Nora's voice was soft, but it shook. "And there was a talking walrus." That would be the general, Iko supposed. "Like I saw in a cartoon."

They met Ben at the door. "This is my friend Ben Harmon. He's going to help us with the doors." Nora eyed him suspiciously, but didn't say anything. Ben opened the doors for them. There was a person missing from the car as they moved through it. The next car was unchanged. They made it back to their own car. Relief lifted Iko's shoulders and she felt as if she could actually take a full breath again.

"This is Miss Nora. She'll be joining us this afternoon." Iko introduced the young girl. "This is Miss Pam."

The artist waved. "Let me get out those crayons and paper like I said. Would you like me to make pictures to fill in or would you like to do that yourself?"

"I'll do it. Thank you."

"And you've met Ben. This is Mr. Serendinski. Mrs. Chattergee. General Clauson. Mr. Gold. Mr. Lewis."

Nora looked at the adults with wide eyes. "You're all awake?"

"Yes. That's why we wanted to ask you to join us."

"I'm sorry that I disturbed you, young lady," the general said. His mustache puffed out as he spoke. Nora smiled shyly at him. "It's a pleasure to meet you."

"Thank you, sir." Her voice was high and clear.

"And what can you tell us about your journey so far today?" Mr Lewis asked with a gentle smile that betrayed his fatherhood more clearly than his handling of Jimmy had at lunch. Nora's smile widened. "We got on the train in Washington. Mother had taken me to see the animals in the zoo and then we went to see the museum with the skeletons of the dinosaurs which was very neat."

Iko sat down and pulled Nora onto her lap. "Then, once we were on the train, Mother sat doing her knitting and I was watching out the window. We passed so many towns. And it looked like we were going through train stations. Daddy said we didn't stop when they train should have stopped. After awhile, there was nothing happening in the towns we were passing through. I thought it was boring. I got out my book, but it was already time for us to go to lunch. Mother and Father took me to the dining car. And there was silver and crystal and real tablecloths! The china even had pictures on it, like I only see at Grandmother's. And we had roasted chicken and peaches for dessert. And we went back to our seats. Mother fell asleep and her yarn rolled away down the aisle. I wound it up so that no one would trip on it.

"And then Father fell asleep. He started snoring so I pushed on his shoulder. He didn't wake up, but he moved his head to the side and stopped making noise. I sat down to read. It was really quiet in the car, because everyone was asleep. I decided to explore a little bit and when I was in the next set of seats, one of the men sitting there disappeared. He was right in front of me and then he was gone. I went back to my seat because that seemed really weird."

"It would," Lewis said with a nod. "And then what happened?"

"More people disappeared. The old Negro man with the tea came through. He gave me a lolly for free because my parents were asleep. He put his fingers to his lips so it would be a secret. It was cherry. I ate it already. I didn't want Mother to wake up and take it away from me. She doesn't think I should have sugar." The little girl shrugged. "I was reading when the talking walrus." She paused. "I'm sorry. I mean General Clauson came through to talk to me. There was no one in the car, but I didn't know him and Mother said not to walk away. Then, Miss Maynard came and offered crayons and cards and that seemed like a lot more fun than sitting and reading or doing my weaving."

"Just so," the general said with a nod. His mustache was twitching in amusement. "And if you'd like we could play a hand of Old Maid or Go Fish? Or you could draw like Miss Pam has been doing."

"I'd like to draw. Thank you."

Pam smiled. She set the drawing pad and crayons on the floor in front of the general and Mrs. Chattergee. It was a good choice, Iko thought. They were old enough to be her grandparents and were exotic enough that they'd be able to keep her attention for the trip. Pam settled down next to Ben once more and curled up under his arm. She poked him in the side. "Cigarette," she demanded. He laughed at her and lit the cigarette for her. She stayed leaning against him as the smoke curled around her face like a gauzy halo.

Iko went to view the pictures. Before she could get there though, Serendinski was in her path. "Don't be like that," he said with a toothy smile. "Talk to me for a minute."

"I would prefer not to."

"Let me apologize for being drunk and for grabbing you."

"It's forgotten," she said. Her back stiffened. She glanced out of the corner of her eye and saw Lewis' hand fisting. She wouldn't be alone if she had to fight him this time.

"And will you sit with me, then?"

She glanced at the empty spots. "I will sit across from you and you will not grab me."

He held his hands up in innocence that she did not believe. Still, Mother always told her to give people second chances. It was the Christian thing to do after all. Grandmother had always stressed that military men were to be obeyed. The camps were gone, but their memory and the habits weren't. "I won't grab you." He sat down in his seat while she took the seat near the window and farthest from him. "You really do look like my Yukio."

"Your Yukio?" Iko prompted.

"She was a girl I knew in Okinawa. I loved her, but she wasn't exactly faithful." He laughed bitterly. "She had to make money, after all. All of the dancing in the world wouldn't have paid the bills for taking care of her parents. Her father was a soldier. He'd lost a hand and an eye in the war."

Iko didn't say a word, but she felt a keen empathy for a young woman who had to support her family. Serendinski looked at her for a long moment. "I didn't always sleep with her went we met. Sometimes I took her out for dates instead. Paid for everything, but I thought she was a nice girl in a bad situation. Not the only one either. The corners were full of whores trying to support families. Some of them were sick, but most of them were young and pretty like you."

She felt her jaw clench. Serendinski wasn't drunk anymore. She hoped that he would actually be bearable.

"She always smelled of talcum powder and make-up. Her lips were painted deep red and she'd wear these American dresses when she was out. When I met her at her room, she would be wearing one of those robe things made of brocade and her clip-clop sandals. I hated that robe. It always meant it would take awhile to get her out of it. Two cups of shitty tea and rice balls that she'd mold into little hearts."

"Did you learn to speak Japanese from her?" Iko asked quietly.

"Nah. Never did really. Spoke this weird half and half thing with her. She knew a little English. I knew a little Jap. We managed for all the big things. Those rice balls always wanted to stick in my throat. She always giggled, this high-pitched thing, when they did."

"Did you say goodbye when you left Okinawa?" Iko asked after he lapsed into silence. She wanted this story ended. She didn't want to think about him grabbing, hurting some young woman who just wanted to send money home to her father.

"I went to see her one night. After she had most of her appointments. It was almost midnight and I'd snuck off base to see her and drink some sake and eat a cheap rice ball. And when I went into her room, she was dead. There was silk tied around her throat from the tie that she used to wear around her waist. Her make up was smeared, but she was laying there so neatly that I didn't, couldn't tell she was dead. I went to touch her and she was still warm to the touch. I kissed her smearing that lipstick on my own mouth, waxy and nasty. And she didn't move. It was then that I realize that this wasn't some game. That she wasn't going to wake up." Revulsion made Iko's breath catch. What sort of man would think that was a game?

He took a gulping breath. He reached for the silver flask at his hip. It glittered like a fish jumping into a lake. He gulped it down without stopping. "Jesus, man. Easy," Ben murmured. He was watching them with sharp eyes. Iko chest felt heavy, like she couldn't breath. Yukio, poor Yukio, she thought.

"I went a little crazy. Smashed the tea cups. Threw the sake against the wall. I broke down like a little baby and cried until the MP's grabbed me. And they just threw me in the brig for being drunk. I was sober too. When I woke up, the commander explained to me that I had gotten drunk and went to see my usual whore who happened to be dead. They found the bastard who did it too. Another Jap. It wasn't even another soldier that did her in. Not a dirty American. One of her own kind wrapped her belt around her throat and pulled tight." He buried his face in his hands.

Iko put her hand to her throat. She could feel something tight. Like her necklace had been pulled back until it bit into the skin of her throat. She blinked rapidly and escaped to the comfort of her seat and the stenopad. Lewis took one look at her and offered his own seat. He took her seat instead. He watched Serendinski like a hawk. Gold put an arm around her and she allowed it. "He shouldn't have put that on you, Miss Maynard. He should have grabbed one of us, if he needed to release all that."

She rested her head on his shoulder. His shoulder was broad and comfortable like her father's. She closed her eyes for just a moment.

"Oh, no you don't. Wake up."

"I'm not asleep."

"Let's keep it that way, then." She sat up. She reached up to straighten her hat. "I think there's room in the luggage room, if you'd like to put your hat there," Lewis offered.

"No, thank you. Thank you for the loan of your shoulder, Mr. Gold."

"You are quite welcome, Miss Maynard." He released her shoulders and her back felt cold.

Nora was explaining her picture to the General and Mrs. Chattergee who had spread out to let her sit between them. "What a lovely blend of colors you've chosen for my scarf."

Iko blinked a bit. She needed to see the picture of Serendinski. It was important, but it could wait. "Would

you like the last of your tea? It's a bit cold, I'm afraid."
Lewis offered the cup.

"Oh yes." She took the cup and sipped. The tightness
in her throat eased. Tea solved most problems, her mother
contended. Iko was now inclined to believe her.

Chapter 7


Pam had closed her eyes again by the time Ben called Iko over. "She's trying to sleep and I can't seem to keep her awake. Will you talk to her?" His voice was tight.

"Maybe you could get your guitar and sing to us?" Iko settled across from Pam with a smile. She peeled off her gloves. She didn't want to stain them anymore than they already were. She accepted the sketchbook with a smile. Pam looked at her through sleepy eyes. Her pupils were widely black. It would seem that her cigarette was more than just tobacco. That was foolish but understandable. Heaven knew, Iko wouldn't mind being a little more relaxed.

The picture on the page made her breath catch. It was Serendinski, that was sure, but he wasn't wearing his crumpled suit, or even the uniform she'd half expected. He was wearing a teeshirt and a leather jacket. His jacket was open exposing a weapon at his side. It was his sneering face that caught her off-guard. She stared at it, her mind spinning out into memories. She'd met him somewhere before. Oh why couldn't she remember where she knew him from. Could it have been one of the camps. Had she seen him as a child? He wasn't that much older, at least in this picture.

"He looks pretty much like himself, don't you think?" Pam asked idly.

"He does." Iko flipped back a page to see Mrs. Chattergee captured in the folds of white fabric as rendered in light and shadow.

"I couldn't resist the patterns. They're fabulous. She tells me it's called a sari and all the women in India wear them. Hers is white because she's a widow."

"Oh, how sad."

"She seems okay with it. Her hair has little streaks of white in it, if you look closely enough. You don't see them mostly because of that gorgeous silk scarf she has. It was a present from her eldest daughter when she came to America."

Iko flipped back one more page. There was Mrs. Chattergee's face. She looked herself, only radiant. There was something other-worldly in her picture. There was more light to her skin, or her eyes, or something. It made Iko think of holy haloes. Or enlightenment. She felt as if she should genuflect in front of her. There were hands around Mrs. Chattergee's holding different objects. Maybe they referred to all the things that she had done in her life. "Why the hammer?"

"For destruction." Pam's voice was soft and dreamy. "And the lightening bolt for anger. And the snake for rebirth and healing. Ask her about the stories of the gods and goddesses. She has a lovely storytelling voice."

"She's a nurse."

"She is. She was a nurse when the English were in charge of India. And she came to America to gather support for the Indian revolution. She worked as a nurse in Morocco with the Red Cross. She's fabulously well-traveled. I don't know if she moved with her husband or if she's older than I think. Take a look at the general. I tried to draw him the way Nora sees him. It's after the drunk-jerk."

"He has his own problems."

"Doesn't bother me that he's tortured and crying for a woman he treated like crap. I think you need to look at the general." The tone of voice sounded like a fortune teller. Iko flipped until she found the walrus version of the general. She giggled and covered her mouth. She didn't want to disturb anyone, or set Serendinski off into another fit. One more and she saw the general as a thin old man. He didn't look like the general she'd met at all. His eyes were small and black and his hair was cut short, even his mustache. He was standing proudly under the banner of the British Raj. Maybe he'd been smaller as a younger man.

Ben settled the guitar on his lap and started to tune it. "I write poetry and song lyrics. But I don't know if anyone here would actually like them, so I'm just going to fool around with some music. You don't mind do you?"

"Not at all. I only play piano. I like music though. Thank you for these. I need to get back to Mr. Lewis and Mr. Gold. To see if there's anything we haven't written up yet." Iko very carefully didn't look at anyone until she was seated.

"So, what are you up to with Miss Pam?" Lewis asked. He raised his brows expectantly.

"She's drawing portraits of the people in the car. I hope you don't mind."

"Is she a very lifelike artist or does she do impressionistic work?"

"I think that depends on your definition of life."

"A politic answer if I've ever heard one," Gold said. "Let us continue with our wool-gathering."

"Information gathering might be a better word for it."

"Could be but I don't believe that." Gold shook his head. "We know very little."

"We know more than we did when this started."

"Station coming," Serendinski announced. He'd moved to the window seat and was looking ahead of them. The car went quiet, hoping against hope that they might hear the brakes engage or feel the shuddering jerk of the train as it pulled to a stop. Iko closed her eyes. She didn't want to see anyone disappear.

Nora's cry caught her attention. She saw that two of the men who'd been sitting with the general's section were gone. Nora was staring at the empty seats with wide eyes. "I want to find Mommy," she said.

"I'll go with you." Nora's hand was warm in Iko's hand. She looked at the bitten nails on her hand and grimaced. It didn't matter who saw them now. She was followed by a quiet Lewis. He held the doors for them. The car with Nora's parents no longer existed. In fact the train itself seemed to have been shortened beyond recognition. The dining car was back though.

"We're not open yet, Miss," the man behind the counter said.

"That's fine. We're simply looking for this young lady's parents."

"Ah. Okay. We'll see you at four for dinner." The man went back to his preparations. They looked through all of the remaining cars, but they didn't find Nora's parents, although they did find her bag with her weaving project and her books. Lewis picked it up and carried it for her without asking. He offered an arm to carry Nora back.

The little girl clambered up into his arms and buried her face in his shoulder as she cried. "I want Mommy."

"I know, sweetheart. I know. We'll keep looking. Maybe they were just in the bathroom."

"Or they're looking for us in our car. I did leave a note." Nora sniffled, but didn't seem to believe them. That was okay; Iko didn't believe herself. She was fairly certain that Lewis didn't believe it either. He handed the bag of little girl entertainments over so that he could open the doors. They made their way through the dining car. "What will the dinner menu look like?"

"There's chicken and pasta and steak, sir. With salad and onion soup."

"Thank you." They entered their own car with a much subdued Nora, sucking on her thumb like a much smaller child. Ben was playing something soft and romantic. It wasn't a lullaby, but it was soothing. His fingers moved over the frets with an ease of motion that made it look as if there was nothing to it. He was plucking the strings like a Spanish player. Pam was sitting on the floor with her sketchbook. She was drawing quick little sketches of his movements. Serendinski looked over at them. His face was pasty and there were red blotches on his cheeks from the alcohol. It was possible he'd been crying.

Lewis sat down with Nora still curled up on him. Gold put a hand over his wrist and squeezed. Lewis turned his hand over and their hands clasped for just a moment. Gold dealt out a hand of solitaire on the seat that had once been occupied by a diligent letter writer. He didn't cheat himself, Iko noticed. She stared out the window. Jimmy and Mrs. Wells were still there. They were supposed to be going to Boston as well, she remembered. "What was the last stop we passed?"

"Newark," Gold said. He glanced significantly at Lewis.

"Did we check the tickets to see if there's actually a correlation between the stops and the tickets?"

"We didn't." General Clauson lifted himself up. He checked the tickets for the men who'd been in their area. "One of them is Newark the others are not." He sat down heavily.

"It would be easier if there were a way to predict these things. I take it you were unsuccessful," Gold said.

"We found her bag, but the car wasn't there. Somehow the luggage is connected to the person. It may take longer to fade away." Iko spoke in a low voice. She didn't want to upset Nora anymore.

"No, Nora, don't go to sleep. You need to stay awake for a little while longer, okay?" Lewis said. He tugged lightly on one of her curls. Nora blinked her eyes rapidly.

She climbed out of his lap and took over Jimmy's seat. She held her bag against her chest and stared out the window. Her face was pale and she continued to suck on her thumb. She wasn't dealing with any of them any longer. She hadn't spoken a word beyond wanting her mother. No one wanted to push her.

Pam looked at them from the center of the aisle. Her eyes were still wide and mostly unfocussed. "Come sit with me and make Ben tell us stories with his guitar," she said to Nora holding out her hand. Nora looked at her. There was a dull sheen on her eyes and her nose was red. She took the offered hand. She and Pam sat on the floor in front of Ben and he nodded at something Pam told him. The music changed to something a little more up-tempo. His voice rose and fell with it, but didn't carry beyond the little group of three.

"Back to work," Gold said. He looked over at the little trio. "It might be kindest to let her sleep. Then, she'll end up with her parents."

"We don't know that. We only know that those who fall asleep disappear," Lewis said. "And I don't think her parents would want us to do anything that increased her chances of disappearing into nothing. What purpose would that serve? If it were my son, I hope that whoever found him would fight until the very last to take care of him. I wouldn't want him to fall asleep and wake up somewhere without me."

"You'd do anything to stay with your son." Gold's voice was small. "Or your wife. I know that. You stayed beyond all hope."

"There's always hope." Lewis didn't seem to believe that statement though. His words trailed up at the end like a half-phrased question. He looked at his friend. "I remember when you fell into the lake at twenty-one. It felt like my heart would stop. It wasn't any different looking at Martha and Joseph in those hospital beds. I wouldn't stop believing until the very last thing had been tried."

"I'm not telling you to give up hope. I was just thinking it might be a mercy. I don't know that what we're heading to will be anything good. The number of missing people outside that window makes me worry that we're not on the right heading. Newark should have more people moving around."

"At this time of day, there should be the beginnings of afternoon drives." Lewis paused. "And I'm still here, for whatever that's worth. I had every intention of getting off here. I thought you were transferring?"

"No, I needed to run up to Boston for some research before heading to New York. There's a professor I wanted to interview."

"What's his name?"

Gold froze. He frowned. "I don't remember. I'm sure I have it written down somewhere. Maybe in my notebook. Or did I have a card?"

"His name is Dr. Milhouse. You were getting information on the communists." Lewis didn't look anywhere but the floor. "But you were to get off at Newark and let me continue on to take the interview."

"Because no one should know that you were there. Yes, I remember now." Gold nodded.

Chapter 8

"What does that mean?" Iko asked. "Why can you remember and he can't?"

"Because I was never actually going to Newark. I was always going to Boston. But I didn't fall asleep. So whatever happened here it wasn't just part of this memory glitch. But can you remember exactly who you were going to meet in Boston? Where were you going to stay?"

"I'll be living on the campus. In the graduate housing until I get my own apartment by the beginning of classes."

"And who were you to meet?" Lewis' eyes drilled into her.

"Miss..." She stopped. She frowned down at her purse. She wanted to open it and pull out her book and hide in it. "Miss Fromme, I believe."

"And what was Miss Fromme going to give you to do?"

"I'm helping to organize the admissions packets and to help with something else. But she was going to give me all the details when I arrived."

"Miss Fromme at which college?" Gold asked.

"M.I.T. My father talked to the dean who said that there was a position there for me."

"And how did your father meet the dean?"

"They served together."

"And where did you get onto the train?" Lewis asked. Her eyes darted between the two men. It felt like a pop-quiz in front of the entire class. Iko's heart-rate jumped.

"Union Station in Washington, DC."

"Do you remember seeing Nora there?"

"No, but I wasn't looking. I was too busy telling my mother not to worry about me and loading my trunk with the help of the porter to think of anyone else."

"Who was in this car when you got here?" Gold asked.

"Ben and Pam. And many of the businessmen." She looked up at him. "Why are you pressing my memory so hard?"

"Because someone needs to be aware of their memories, as I obviously may not be. I don't recall where I got onto the train, only where I am supposed to go," Gold stated.

"What is the last thing you recall then?" Iko sat up. She met his eyes evenly.

"I remember getting a ticket from my boss for this assignment. Normally, I would have been in New York, but I don't believe I was. And I don't recall why Mr. Lewis was here."

"I was in DC visiting you," Lewis informed him. He frowned.

"I thought you worked for the *New York Times*, Mr. Gold?" Iko frowned.

"I do. But I am based in DC. I attend briefings at the White House and send my stories out by wire. I attend briefings at Congress. I even interview common people in the area about the government so that I get better stories than any of the slackers who live in New York. I'm ahead of the curve, you see. I wouldn't have it any other way." Gold seemed pleased with himself and she gave him a smile. There was a chance that he was telling the truth even.

"And I recall that I have a bag besides the one at my feet, but I don't recall what I've packed into it."

"Then perhaps we should go into the luggage and find out. Just to make you feel more steady," Lewis said. Gold stood to do just that. He prodded Lewis up into the center of the aisle and into the luggage room with taunting, long fingers.

"If you poke me one more time, I will break your finger," Lewis hissed. Iko debated following them for a moment, but couldn't contain her curiosity. She wanted to see what was in the luggage room. Lewis was standing in front of three rows of metal shelves, trying to determine which black trap was his. The camel colored one could only belong to Mr. Gold. He pulled it from the shelf and poked through it. There was a traveling trunk covered with stickers that was likely Mrs. Chattergee's. The two duffle-bags on the bottom row were probably Ben and Mr. Serendinski's. Lewis pulled out his suitcase. He flipped it open and stopped, staring into its depths.

Iko looked down into it. There was a suit and tie neatly folded onto one side with a pair of shiny shoes. The other side held a selection of books and three boxes of what was labeled as bullets and a gun. There were two notebooks and a tape recorder as well. "Well, I hope you have a bottle of liquor in there to. Just to make it a complete sweep." Gold commented.

Lewis snorted out a laugh. He felt under the suit and came up with a bottle of amber liquid. He handed it to his friend and closed the suitcase up again. "Maybe it's for the best that I don't remember everything that's in this bag. What do you say, Miss Maynard?"

"I think that you should tell everyone that you're an undercover private detective. It might ease their minds."

That managed to get a smile out of him. He put the case back onto the shelf. "I think that we'll leave knowledge of that to later. Right now, I think I'll dump the dregs of my coffee out the window and have a shot of something familiar and biting."

"Do you think alcohol is the best bet?"

"Well, I won't offer any to Serendinski, given he didn't offer his flask, but everyone else is more than welcome to join me." Lewis offered the alcohol around.

Only Ben and the general took him up on the offer. Mrs. Chattergee shook her head at their antics. "Come sit with me, Mr. Lewis."

"Of course, ma'am." He sat down next to her and savored his drink as they fell into light conversation.

Gold saluted Iko with his own cup of scotch. "I admire your fortitude."

"I dislike the taste of alcohol," she told him. "And why don't you check your own bags? Maybe you can find the information on the professor."

"No, it's fine. Lewis told me everything I needed to know about the assignment."

"Do you take him on your assignments often?"

"We tend to be moving in the same directions more often than not. He's an editor after all and I can always use a good editor. He doesn't work for the Times. He works for McMillan. He doesn't spend that much time in New York though. He travels up and down the coast finding interesting professors to coerce into writing textbooks for subjects he doesn't know yet. He collects them." Gold smiled into his cup. Iko looked at him.

"You've known him for a long time then?"

"Seems like I've known him forever. I don't know exactly when we met. I think we were twelve maybe?"

"Forever and a day," she laughed.

"Exactly. I remember distinctly putting worms into his lunch and him pushing me into puddles in retaliation. So maybe we were younger, but I don't think so."

"Were you in the war?"

"Not in the way you'd think. They wanted our brains more than our hands."

"I think you could have made a good soldier."

"Oh, no doubt. I think there are a lot of people who'd make good soldiers who simply didn't join up or weren't drafted. And where did you spend the war?"

"At a camp in the midwest. There was a windmill. And there were so many people in such a small area. Mother and I were lucky enough that when Father came back from the war, we had someplace to stay. There were many who didn't. Their businesses went out or their jobs were replaced."

"Interred then? How old were you?"

"Seven. I was seven. My brother was two. He didn't really remember before the camp, so it wasn't so hard for him. And I was better off than the girls who were older than I was. We should decide what to do about dinner. The dining car is back in service."

"And back in existence then? That would have been nice to tell us."

"We didn't think of it. I don't want to go alone. I don't think just one or two of us should go either. I think we should all go at once. We'll see anyone who's awake then, I think. If we stay for the full time."

"Good thinking." Gold raised his voice. "Is everyone content to go to dinner together?" There were nods of affirmation. Even Serendinski nodded. Iko promised herself that she would not sit near him. Ben finished up his song-story. "Think we should go down now? It's open right?"

"Dom?" Lewis prompted.

Gold looked at his pocket-watch "It's quarter after four."

"Yes. They were opening at four according to the cook we ran into." There was a moment of scrabbling as everyone got to their feet. It was decided that General Clauson would lead and that Lewis would bring up the rear with Gold. Iko managed to get between Pam and Mrs. Chattergee rather than be near Serendinski. Ben carried Nora.

The dining car seemed more spectacular than it had at lunch. The cloths were a rich burgundy and the crystal of the glasses sparkled in the soft light from the oil lamps. The lamp's delicate hurricanes glowed romantically, despite the fact it was still light out. There were more forks than Iko had ever seen. They were seated at small tables throughout the car.

Serendinski sat down across from her. "Peace. Please. Let me buy you dinner. I won't try anything. I just don't want to sit with the happy couple and their new child or the old man and the foreign woman."

"You seemed to believe that I was a foreign woman earlier."

"I was drunk. I can hold my tongue and a civil conversation. I promise."

"If you try anything, I'll have Mr. Lewis stab you with a steak knife."

Lewis glanced over at the sound of his name. His brows raised in question. He hadn't settled in his seat yet. Iko shook her head. She could handle dinner. Serendinski was attempting to make amends.

"My word on it." They ordered dinner. She had tea. He had wine. "I don't remember getting on the train, just that I have to get to Boston to see my mother."

"Were you already drunk?"

"No. God no. I don't drink before noon. It's an old rule, but it helps. Keeps me from being completely blotto the whole day. The hangovers are willing to kill." He was quiet until the food arrived on the table and she let the silence lie between them. The man had confessed to finding his lover dead in her bedroom. She didn't like him any more than she had before, but at least he was something that wasn't completely alien. He was grieving still. He picked at his chicken. "Was I on the train when you got on?"

"I don't remember. I didn't notice you."

"I could have gotten on in Norfolk maybe. Richmond. Somewhere down Virginia way. Maybe I'd know the area better that way. Yukio wasn't the only woman I knew who got killed over there." The abrupt topic change made her jump.

"And for some reason you hate them all."

"They left me!" He winced at the sound of his own voice. "I'm sorry. I'm so sorry. I didn't mean to hurt you."

She looked down at the bruises on her wrist. "I don't believe that."

His eyes flashed something cold and dangerous. "Are you calling me a liar?"

"Yes." She lifted her chin. Her heart felt like it was going to beat out of her chest. She couldn't stop herself from baiting him. Did she want him to lash out? He threw a glass across the room.

The server was there and instant later. "Sir?" The man's voice was completely neutral, but Iko could see the anger that he was hiding. "If you persist in this behavior I'll have to ask you to leave the car. You're disturbing the other guests."

"Right. Right. Won't happen again." He took a deep breath. "Could I get a cup of black coffee?"

"Yes, sir."

Iko's hand trembled and knocked her fork against her plate. She was suddenly very aware of the keen attention that Lewis and Gold were paying to their table.

Serendinski couldn't see them, but Lewis was in her sightline and Gold could turn around and have a hand on him within a moment's notice. They wanted her to get information out of him. He would talk to her. How much worse could his answers get? "Did you kill any of them?"

He blinked at her. "I don't know what you're talking about."

"Did you hurt them? Did you beat them? You seemed shocked that when you found her dead they didn't accuse you of her death. Were you known for hurting women?"

His hand fisted around his coffee cup. He dropped his eyes to his plate. He picked at the meal there for a few minutes before he answered. "I might have batted Yukio around a few times, but I never left marks. I never hurt her that bad."

"Did you hurt any of them that badly? Did you leave marks like this on your paid companions?" She chose the words carefully. She didn't want to set him off into a rant about prostitutes and whores and how she was one again.

"A few of them. It didn't mean anything."

"Have you ever killed a woman?" she asked bluntly. Her hand rose to her throat. She could feel the echoes of tightness there.

His eyes widened. He stared at the flame of the oil lamp rather than looking at her. "I can't remember," he whispered. "Isn't that something you should remember?"

"Yes, yes it is."

Chapter 9

The walk back to the car was frightening. There was only one passenger left in the car just before the dining car. Nora clutched Pam's hand until the artist winced. Iko put a steadying hand on the little girl's shoulder. They made it back to their car with no true issues. Serendinski hid away in his corner, not meeting anyone's eyes. He stared out at the countryside, seemingly unconnected to the rest of the world. Iko sat down in her usual seat, but the men across from her didn't actually say anything to her. Gold was staring down at his hands as if he'd never seen them before.

"I remember holding my wife in my arms as she died," Lewis said quietly. "I remember my son dying in a hospital bed. And I remember Gold dying when we were no more than twenty-one. How can that be?"

Iko looked up from her contemplation of the black stains on her dress. Her eyes were wide. Lewis was looking only at the floor. He lifted his head to regard her. "I don't know," she said after a moment of silence that seemed too heavy to be real.

"I don't remember dying at all." Gold's voice was soft. "I remember working on articles, and running up and down the coast for stories. I remember traveling to France to interview the veterans there about the differences in veteran's returns. I remember doing all of those things. How can I remember more than 15 years worth of memories when he remembers me dead? Or am I not the same boy who died?"

"No, you are the same man, but that doesn't mean that you died. It just means that he thinks you did. He was told you did, but that doesn't mean you actually did."

"I remember teaching his son slight of hand. I remember his wedding and kissing his bride on the lips just to see her family pull back in shock and his start laughing. I nearly kissed him too, but he was quick enough to push me off on the maid of honor." Gold leaned back.

"I remember that. I remember thinking that you'd scandalized my family enough already. And I remember editing your first articles so that they sounded coherent and I remember your first job. I remember you pulling coins from Joseph's ear. I remember you entertaining him with card tricks when he had the chicken pox."

"Then obviously he didn't die. Or if he did, he was saved. It was just the emotion that scared you and you held onto the memory." Iko said it as if it were truth. If she believed it, maybe they could too.

"I like that explanation," Gold gave her a wry smile. "I think I shall keep it and adapt it as necessary."

"What's the count?" Ben queried.

"We've lost two more from the back seats," Clauson answered.

Iko turned her attention back to her hands and the bitten off fingernails. She looked at the nicks on the back of her hand from working in the garden and the dark ring of bruises that circled her wrist like a macabre bracelet. Pam crossed over to sit in the window seat near Gold. She had her sketchbook. She focussed on drawing the mother and child asleep on the seats. They were a constant reminder that they had no clue what was going to happen. Lewis reached across to touch Jimmy' pinwheel and set it spinning. Pam's eyes lit up at the motion.

Mrs. Chattergee took a deep breath. She put a hand to her chest. Iko was immediately drawn to the action. The general sat up a bit more straight. "My dear? What is it?"

"My heart is fluttering. Perhaps it is merely too much tea." She pressed her hand tighter to her chest. "Perhaps it is something else. There's no way to tell."

Iko crossed the aisle to take her pulse and look at her eyes. She wanted so badly to beg some distant god to make this not happen. She wanted to believe that there was some reason beyond what she knew to what was happening here. She lifted Mrs. Chattergee's wrist and counted her pulse using the little silver watch that the woman wore.

She smiled kindly at Iko. "Here, Miss Maynard. Take my watch. You will have more need of it than I."

"Mrs. Chattergee. I couldn't it's far too expensive."

"Nonsense. I insist. I won't be using it much longer. I am nearing the end of my life. You are still young." She pressed the watch into Iko's hand with both of hers. Her smile was soft. "It is well. I will be with my husband and we will watch the mandala turn."

Iko swallowed hard. The general drew her to his side. "I'll look after her," he promised. "I won't let her sleep just yet." His mustache drooped. "She has yet to finish her story and Scheherazade cannot rest until her story is complete." He shot Mrs. Chatergee a sly glance.

She chuckled and patted his hand where it rested between them. "Indeed. I shall finish my tale, Emperor." They fell into that rolling language that was strange to Iko's ears, yet made her feel that she should smile because they were so obviously enjoying themselves.

She sat back in her seat. Pam looked at her. Her eyes were not nearly as dreamy. Iko raised her brows. "I've had some coffee. I'm not nearly as mellow as I was. It's a shame. It feels good to be so undone." She turned the sketchbook around and Iko stared at it.

Lewis gasped. "That is not Mrs. Wells."

"Isn't it?" Pam's voice was mild. "This is what I see when I draw her."

Lewis' hand shook, as he reached out. It was Gold who took the book though. He stared for a long time at the picture. "It looks just like Martha." He said quietly. He looked at the sleeping woman. "She does look a bit like her, I suppose. The charcoal simply enhances it." He flipped the pages back until he reached the beginning. He looked through them slowly. "You love Ben a great deal."

"I do. I love him more than anything."

"Enough to give up everything to be with him."

"I'm not saying that I don't love the art, but yes, I joined the movement to be with him. To support him. To love him. And to travel the world. We have things to see and people to meet and there is so much we've not done yet. I don't want to ever give it up."

"And you're free."

"Oh yes. I'm free. Not completely. No one ever is. But I am free to love who I want, to be who I want."

"Free to be looked down on. Free to be ignored," he challenged.

"Ben treats me better than that. Ben treats me as if I'm his world and that's all that matters to me."

"You lost your child."

"You're reading between the lines."

Gold turned the sketchbook to face Pam. "I'm reading nothing. It's all here in the small child curled in his arms."

"That's his guitar."

"It's much more than that. Did he hurt you?"

"No. It wasn't Ben. It was a cop who thought I was open to being bought. He punched me when I told him off. He picked us up on vagrancy charges even though we had our train tickets and were in the station." Tears welled up in her eyes. "It hurt so badly that I didn't know that it was more than the punch until the blood started and hit the floor. He freaked out at that. There was a female secretary. A nurse maybe. She screamed at him and then took me someplace quiet. Away from all of them. Ben followed. He told them we were married, but we couldn't afford rings. They had to believe it."

"And what happened."

"We got on the train in New Orleans and started our grand adventure to Boston." A single tear tracked down her cheek. "We're going to start over in Boston. Be bohemians in a new state. Maybe some place where the cops aren't after us for looking different."

"Some place closer to the sea."

"Yes. A harbor like home. A place where no one knows us. Where I'm just Pam and he's Ben and no one can throw us into prison for being ourselves."

There was something in Gold's eyes that made Iko bite her lip. There was something she hadn't understood in the conversation. What she had understood was enough. "Oh, Pam." She enfolded the artist into her arms. Pam's arms came around her waist, clutching to the back of her dress. She sobbed once and then was quiet. She didn't loosen her grip though. Her tears were hot as they soaked through the silk of Iko's shoulder. She pulled Iko into her lap, which seemed to be a rather backwards way to do things, but if she felt better than that was it.

Nora came to crawl into Lewis' lap with drooping eyes. "Is Miss Pam okay?"

"She will be. It will take a little time." Nora tucked her head onto his shoulder.

"Mommy's not coming back for me is she?"

"She will if she can. Believe that Nora. She didn't want to leave you. She wouldn't have left you if she had any choice in the matter."

Nora nodded. She blinked. "I'm really tired."

"Can you stay awake for a little bit longer? Mr. Gold has some card tricks he'd like to show you." Gold set the sketchbook on Iko's seat. He started by making cards appear from Nora's ears and nose. And then from behind her knee. Then, he started showing off his ability to shuffle the cards. He cut them one handed, fanned them, made them walk and much more.

Pam's fingers and arms loosened their grip. "I've messed up your dress," she said. Her voice was a harsh croak.

"Dresses clean." Iko fished out a white hankie from her purse. "Here."

"At least I don't have any more mascara on," she laughed. It was a watery sound.

"Pick a card, Darling," Gold said, holding the cards out the her. Pam took one. "Memorize it. Now, slip it back into the pack." He did a few dazzling movements with the cards and then pulled one out. Is this your card?" Pam nodded and smiled, though her eyes were still wounded.

He did the same trick with Nora instead. Iko picked the sketchbook up and looked through it idly. She flipped to the last page. The one where Mrs. Wells and Jimmy were sleeping. She didn't see any differences between the real thing and the picture. Maybe it was simply self-protection that Lewis didn't see the resemblance to his wife. It would hurt him too much if he did.

She flipped back to the very beginning to look at the pictures there. They were mostly of Ben and a few of the train stations they were in. There was a self-portrait as well. Pam was wearing flat shoes, tight black pants and a black sweater. Her hair was loose around her shoulders and she was smoking a cigarette. There was an impression of words in the smoke. Iko squinted, trying to make them out. She didn't know what they said, but they seemed important.

"I am not afraid to carry on. I'm not afraid to walk alone," Pam whispered. "It was something my mother said when my father died. She promised she was going to be fine. That was a laugh. She died not a year later. I think it was a broken heart."

"Love can do that to you," Lewis commented. He was tickling Nora's nose with the end of her ponytail while Gold reorganized the cards.

"And did you carry on after your wife?" Pam looked at him with a challenge in her eyes.

"Not very well. Not particularly happily or healthily or any of the things that I did before she died. But I did survive it. I found something else to devote my time to and it worked out well enough. I've got my work. I've got Gold."

Gold smiled in relief. Iko had to feel for him.

"Oh, my dear," the general said quietly. He laid Mrs. Chattergee out on the floor and covered her face with her scarf. Everyone's head turned to face them.

Chapter 10

Clauson pushed himself off of the floor with the seat. Lewis caught him under the elbow to steady him. "I'm fine, son," the old man protested. "Just this knee that acts up sometimes. Shot in the knee when I was climbing down the trellis behind my lover's house." He grinned to show either that it was a joke or that a young man like Mr. Lewis should understand the accomplishment that it was. He settled back in his seat. "Ain't seemly to keep her out like this. By all rights, she'll want a pyre, but the officials might have something to say about that."

"Somehow I don't think the officials are the most of our worry."

"Is Mrs. Chattergee sleeping now too?" Nora's voice was wavering. It was as though she could tell something was different, but she wasn't old enough to truly grasp it.

Pam took her hand. "No, sweetheart. Mrs. Chattergee won't be waking up ever. She's already gone. Nothing can hurt her now."

"Oh."

Ben started playing a song. It was soft and slow. He spoke words to it, but they were too soft to hear.

"Speak up, son. Some of us are deaf," Clauson chided him. "If you're going to sing a lament, do it right." Ben huffed out a laugh, but he raised his voice. The lament was soft and sweet and in what Iko finally identified as French. She settled back. She gripped the silver watch until it cut into the side of her hand. The sharp pain reminded her that she was still alive and that she now had the responsibility of looking after the rest of the people in the car. She swallowed and put the watch on over the bruises. Everything she'd received so far in one place.

"We should move her somewhere," Serendinski said. He was pacing in the small area of the seats he'd claimed. It was three steps up and three steps back to the window. He looked like a child's toy that was malfunctioning. "We can't leave a dead body in the middle of the car."

"We will move her when we know there's somewhere to move her to." Gold's voice was sharp and Serendinski jerked to a stop to glare at him.

"It's not right to leave her there."

"Why not?" Iko asked. "Death is part of life."

Lewis looked at her with a line between his eyes. He wasn't actually frowning, but he seemed confused with her statement. "Iko, did she say something to you?"

"Just that all would be well. She'd be with her husband and watching the mandala spin. She didn't seem to be worried about dying. She seemed content."

"She was content," the general said quietly. "She was an extraordinary woman and it was a blessing for me to have met her again."

"Again?"

"It was years ago. I was still in the service and she was working on the lines. She was a nurse. She was young and pretty, rather than old and pretty. She was married. She was the most exotic woman I'd ever fallen for. I was so young and stupid back then." He chuckled. "This was well before any of you were born of course. I learned Hindi just to be able to talk to her. It would never come to anything. I knew that, even back then. I just wanted to know her. To know her mind."

He paused to resettle himself and to massage his leg. "And I did learn from her. I learned how to talk to the troops. I learned how to navigate the markets. And when I went back to Britain I supported independence, simply because I knew the men that had worked for me and with me. And I knew her. I wanted her to know that I'd listened." He smiled. "And I got to see her one more time before we both died. Yes, this wasn't a painful passing for her. She will spin the wheel and be back in the world or she'll meet up with her husband again and be happy in the world beyond this one."

"I'm glad for you both." Iko kept her voice steady. She was starting to suspect that there was a reason beyond what any of them knew to who was asleep and who was awake. She shook Mrs. Wells shoulder, just to see if it would do any good this time. Jimmy's pinwheel slipped from his grasp and fell to the carpet. It lay there against the dried blood red of the floor. She picked it up and spun it with a breath.

Lewis' eyes widened. He hurried to check that the two were still breathing. He let go of a shaky breath. "I don't know why I'm so scared to lose them. They're not my family. I just don't want to lose anyone else I know." He let out a small laugh. "I don't think I can ignore loss anymore. I don't know that I'll be able to survive it."

Gold fanned his cards out. "Pick a card."

Lewis drew a card. He snorted. "King of hearts."

"Suicide King."

"Lucky card."

"They're all lucky. It means that we're still here to read them. Let's help the general figure out the right way to lay her out. We can clean out a shelf in the luggage room and make her a bier."

"Right. Iko, why don't you see to clearing the back section with Ben and we'll put all the luggage there. I really don't think it matters where anyone's sitting these days."

"I'll do it." Serendinski said. "Ben can keep playing songs to entertain Nora."

"Iko?"

"Yes, that will be fine. I'll simply point."

"Okay, then."

Iko took a breath and held it. She released it. "Please don't touch me."

"I won't." He held up a hand in pledge. "On my honor, whatever there is of it. I won't touch you."

She nodded her acceptance and led the way to the final rows of seats. She directed and helped move the smaller bags to the row across the way. There were only three people left there. "Should I get the Mrs. and her kid?"

"No. I think that will upset Mr. Lewis," she said quietly.

"Okay. I'll, I'll go see if they need help hauling the bags down here."

Iko stepped into the sleeping row. She studied the men there. They were all of an age. The oldest was no more than twenty-five. The youngest was her age. She stepped forward and closed her eyes. She didn't smell any alcohol on them, so she was pretty sure they hadn't passed out from that. She straightened the one on the left, so that his head wasn't at such an uncomfortable looking angle. She looked at the bag at his feet and opened it. It wouldn't matter in the end and she might find something to help them. There were three scholarly magazines and a notebook. She flipped open the notebook. Mr. Harold Anderson. There was a sketch of mechanical device on the front cover. An engineer, she decided. She tucked the notebook back into his bag. The next briefcase didn't bring anything interesting either. The last one produced a yo-yo. "I'm just going to borrow this. If you wake up, I'll give it back to you," she promised the sleeping man. She could teach Nora to use it when she started to fade in an hour or so. That might be enough to keep her awake.

The steamer trunks were placed into place between the seats. There were four of them, including hers. She thought that maybe these men were going back to school. That these were their school things. The plain suitcases went on top of those. The two hatboxes and the dufflebags and the guitar case went onto the seats proper. "All right then, sir. We're ready to move her. Any suggestions?" Lewis asked.

"Cross her arms over her chest. And lift with your knees not your backs." General Clauson's voice was steady.

"Yes, sir." Gold and Lewis lifted her awkwardly and moved her to the luggage room, trailing soiled cotton. They laid her on the lowest shelf. Iko tucked the cotton up around her feet and made sure that the scarf covered her face properly. Serendinski was working with the towels from the bathroom to clean up the spill in the middle of the floor. He was scowling. Iko washed her hands in the bathroom. She wiped her hands on her skirt, not caring enough to find something else anymore.

Pam was trying to keep Nora awake, but it was a losing battle. The little girl had held out until almost eight thirty. They should be in Boston now. Iko peered into the deepening twilight. She could see the occasional streetlight, but the streets were abandoned.

"We should have reached Boston," Lewis' voice was quiet as he echoed her thoughts. "Of course, who knows what route we're actually on now. We've missed so many stations, there's no reason to think that we might not have missed a turn off or two." He sounded tired. "I think we should have used a higher shelf," he murmured. "The general is not looking good."

"Get another glass of scotch into him," Pam said.

"I'll offer it."

"Don't bother. Our sailor's already appropriated it. He's through half of what was left," Gold stated.

Lewis' head snapped to the side. "That little bastard. Although, anyone who can gulp it down like that probably has a need for it. Good God."

"We can only hope he drinks himself to sleep."

"No, I don't wish that on him." Iko's voice was firm. "As long as he doesn't become violent, we'll be good. If he does." She stopped. "If he does, I expect that Mr. Lewis will shoot him for me."

"We'll stop him. Never fear." Gold gave her an extravagant bow. "I do wish I were a bit drunk though. It would make whatever comes next a little less traumatic."

"Somehow I question that." Lewis settled back into his seat. "Is that a yo-yo? Miss Maynard, have you been snooping?"

"I have. Do you know any tricks? My little brother knows all sorts of tricks."

"I haven't tried in years. Let me see. It may take me a few minutes to get my wrist working again."

Iko picked up the pinwheel. She looked at Jimmy. He wouldn't notice it missing. When he woke up, she could give it back to him.

"I think we should check the luggage. See if our sleeping beauties were kind enough to have any alcohol to make things interesting." Gold stood to suit action to word.

"You can pester Ben to share his stash."

"That is not my favorite poison. General, do you mind if we look through the provisions?"

"Not at all my boy. Have fun. If you can't get the locks undone, let me know. I used to be a fair hand with a lock-pick."

Gold sketched him a salute. He opened the top suitcase. "Miss Maynard, would you be so kind as to assist me. Do you think Miss Nora would like a few scarves to dress up with?"

"She might," Iko allowed. "Anything that might keep her entertained and awake is a good idea. I know, Nora, dear, would you like to play pirate and look for buried treasure in the suitcases?"

"Oh! Yes." She hurried down the aisle with a lot more energy than she'd shown for about an hour now. Gold dangled scarves out for her to grab and try on. She wrapped them around her neck and arms. They found a picture of Mrs. Wells' husband and Iko put a hand to her mouth to restrain the tears. The thought that they might never see each other again broke her heart. Gold put it aside. He opened up the next case and found nothing particularly interesting.

"Good lord these boys are boring, don't you think, Miss Nora?" The little girl giggled at his exaggerated eye roll. "Oh, now this might be fun." He found a small book of puzzles. "For you, Miss Maynard." She accepted it with a smile.

They moved onto the large trunk with its traveling stickers. "This should be a bit more fun, don't you think? There might be treasure in this one."

Nora giggled. He opened it with a flick of his penknife. "Do you have much experience in opening luggage, Mr. Gold?" Iko teased.

"I've done my share of losing my keys," he volleyed back.

When they were done scavenging, they had lipstick and bangles for Nora to play with. There were magazines for the rest of them to read. And there was one small bottle of absinthe and one bottle of scotch to share around. The general took a sip of the undiluted absinthe, much to the shock of his seatmates. "Don't look at me like that, kids. I was drinking absinthe when you lot were in diapers."

Lewis laughed. The lights flickered.

Cherry Blossom Express

Chapter 11

Everyone in the car froze. They all looked up. This was the first time there had been even the vaguest hint that the lights might not last out the trip. "Do you think the dining car is still available?"

Iko checked her watch. "I don't know what time they stop serving drinks. They seem to be on schedule."

"We'll risk it. We'll need the lights just in case we lose the ones here. Sam, are you with me?"

"Let me get a box to carry them in." He dumped Mrs. Wells hats out onto the top of the suitcases. "We'll be back in a flash." He gave Iko a smile that was more like a grimace. She sat down and folded her hands over the puzzle book. She really should try to fill it out. Instead, she lifted a finger to her mouth and chewed on the nail.

"You shouldn't do that. It's bad for your fingers," Nora informed her solemnly.

"Did your mother tell you that? It sounds just like what my mother used to tell me."

"She did. She also painted my nails with varnish. It tastes really bad."

"I'll have to try that." She pulled her gloves on instead. "This was my mother's solution."

Nora smiled. She handed her a pink scarf. "This will match your dress. You should have it."

"Thank you." Iko tied it around her throat like a girl scout scarf. Nora nodded, satisfied with that. She retreated to Pam's side to play with the bangles and bakelight bracelets that had filled one corner of Mrs. Wells' bags. Serendinski's eyes fastened on the scarf around her neck. He shivered as he stared at it. He wasn't doing anything but staring. She told the butterflies in her stomach to calm down.

They didn't listen.

She swallowed hard against the anxiety that was building in her chest. She untied the scarf and tied it around her bag instead and felt instantly better. She reached to rub at her neck. She was swallowing more easily now. Serendinski's eyes drifted back to his reflection in the dark glass.

The general massaged his shoulder. He sighed heavily. He handed the bottle of absinthe to Pam and retired to the lavatory. Iko opened the puzzle book and tried to concentrate on the words. Her eyes swam. She was so tired of trying to stay awake. Her head nodded down.

The lavatory door opened. She jerked her head up. The general made his unsteady way to the luggage room. She bit her lip. He was saying his own private goodbyes then. She watched the door, hoping that Lewis and Gold would hurry up with the hurricane lamps. The lights flickered again placing them into darkness for nearly twenty seconds before snapping back on. The door between the cars opened in that darkness and she was instantly, completely awake.

"It's just us," Gold announced. "We come bearing gifts of light. The staff was very accommodating when we explained that there was trouble with the lights in our car. And they once again promised to send a porter."

"Oh, the mysterious and non-existent porter will be the answer to all of our prayers," Ben stated. "We haven't seen one since before this began. The staff seemed normal though?"

"They act as if absolutely nothing out of the ordinary is happening and it's actually disconcerting. In the face of such pure belief that everything is all right and that there's nothing wrong, it had me doubting my own eyes. I can't imagine what they might be able to do if they had a bit more time." Gold rubbed the side of his head as though he had a headache.

"We'll light one and leave it on the steamer trunks. Then, if the lights do go out we'll be able to get to it and light the others." Lewis set the box down carefully. "Ben, can I borrow your lighter?"

The musician tossed it across the car and Lewis caught it easily. He lit the wick on one of the lamps. It felt as if the group had released a held breath all at once. The tension was something they hadn't noticed until it was gone. "Where's the general gone?"

"He's in the luggage room with Mrs. Chattergee."

"That dog," Gold murmured into Lewis' ear. Iko knew she wasn't supposed to have heard it and kept her face straight.

Lewis returned Ben's lighter to him. "Sir? Are you okay?" He knocked on the door of the luggage room. He got no reaction. "Sir?" He pushed the door open. "Oh, damn it."

Iko rushed to his side. She knew she had no more than first aid training from school, but she had to see if she could help him. The man was beyond help. The blue tinge of his face and lips told her that. She stepped forward and ran into the steady arm that Lewis had extended across the doorway. "No, don't go nearer. See those bubbles at his lips? He's taken some kind of poison, I think. We shouldn't get too close to it."

Iko stepped back, uncertain. "How do you even know that?"

"I read a lot of mystery novels?"

She raised her brows. "Are you asking me or telling me that?"

"It is a reasonable answer."

"And your gun?"

"I like to target shoot when I have the opportunity. There's no law barring me from carrying it." He smiled at her. "I'll explain in a moment." He closed the door and bent his head to rest against it. She realized that he was praying. It must be nice to have faith like that, she thought. She had gone to church, but it had never meant anything to her. Mother and Grandmother lived by the rules it laid out to them and she listened because she was a good girl. Though, the more she talked to Pam, the less she believed all they'd taught her. She retreated to her seat. Serendinski was leaning against the window now. He watched her go by with half-lidded eyes. He cradled the bottle against his chest like a teddy bear. He bared his teeth at her. The fear grew in her stomach again.

She sat down and looked at the empty seats where the general and Mrs. Chattergee had been sitting. In the window backed by the night, she could see her face. There was a smudge of charcoal on her nose and there was more on her throat that made it look like she had more bruises. She swallowed against the fear that hollowed her eyes. Her skin seemed paler than usual in the strange reflection. She could see trees against the sky and the faint glow of far away lights. They could be anywhere now. As Lewis said, how would they know if they had missed a turn-off?

Gold poured a shot of scotch into her tea mug. "You look like you could use this."

She gave him a wan smile. She lifted the alcohol to her lips. It smelled strange and pricked the inside of her nose. She sipped it and felt the burn like mouthwash across her tongue and then down her throat making the muscles there spasm. The burn pushed past the fear that was caught there. She felt it flow down her throat and into her stomach. She didn't grimace, but the flavor was strong enough to make her teeth ache. She took a larger sip and the process happened once more. The muscles in her neck relaxed of their own volition. The anxiety in her stomach only grew. She knew this feeling.

Lewis settled in his seat. "I'll take a shot of that."

Gold provided it. Lewis passed the bottle to Pam when she held her hand out. Iko regarded the two men. "I think you owe me an explanation?"

Lewis gave her a half smile. "I was in the war, just not in the military sense. They sent me into Germany. As a reporter who was following the troops."

She blinked at him, feeling fuzzy headed. That didn't make sense unless, unless Pam's pictures were correct and Lewis was older than he looked. She granted the answer. Her eyes drifted back to her reflection. Lewis dove forward only to have Gold catch him and hold him back. Mrs. Wells and Jimmy flickered away into the night. Lewis picked up the pinwheel. He moved to the seat by the window and held it out to catch the wind. Iko let herself sink into the windmill rhythm.

Chapter 12

It was Pam who came up with the next suggestion. "We should take whatever we can from the sleepers now before they fade away. Obviously, once we have it, it doesn't disappear with them." She gestured at the colorful scarves and the bracelets that were stacked into a veritable city of towers.

"I'll do it," Gold offered. He stood and went to regard the sleepers. The last three that they had in the car at least. He quickly opened their jackets. He tossed anything of value, wallets, keys, watches, pens, and more over the top of the seat.

Iko squeaked and ducked out of the way. Lewis laughed at her as she straightened her hat. She stuck her tongue out at him. He sorted through the wallets tossing back anything that didn't look promising. He didn't keep any of the money and he didn't bother with any of the ID cards. He only kept tangible things. Pens, rings, anything that would make a toy or keep them fed.

There was a candy bar that flew over the top and a pack of mints that Iko claimed. She set the candy aside for later. They might need it if the dining car didn't reappear. The haul was slim. "I'm going to forage. Will you come with me?"

Lewis looked at Gold. "As if there's truly a question." He found a suitable satchel to put over his shoulder and they went off through the front door to where the first class car used to be.

"Where are you going?" Iko demanded. No one had gone toward first class in hours.

"To see if we can reach the engineer."

"Take my flashlight," Pam said. She dug into her bag to find it. "It might not last very long," she apologized.

"Any light is better than trying to do this in the dark." She gave them a smile. Her eyes seemed perfectly clear although she and Ben had been sharing the absinthe. No one else could stomach it.

Iko watched the men's backs as they were swallowed by the dark between the cars. Serendinski whispered between the seats. "I remember. I did kill a woman once." Her back stiffened. "She was young and pretty like Yukio when I first met her. She had laughing eyes and perfectly straight stockings. She was a student at the college near the base I was on. I met her out for drinks one night and I strangled her with her scarf. It was blue and gold and had a little anchor on it as if it actually belonged to the Navy. She shouldn't have gone for drinks with me."

"No one should drink with you, Mr. Serendinski." She thought her voice came out level, but she wasn't sure. "I think you've had enough to drink today."

"No I haven't not nearly enough. I can still hear her struggling to breath as I hold the scarf. Maybe if I drink enough, it'll go away."

"Maybe if you give yourself up to the authorities the memory will leave you in peace."

"What authorities? All there is are the five of us. Seven if you count the two fags who went looking for supplies. No one to save us. No one to damn us. Just the train and the dark and the memories. God, I hope they bring more to drink."

"Stop drinking, Mr. Serendinski. You're perfectly charming when you're sober. Well, more charming than you are drunk." She left him to that side of the car and went to sit with Pam and Nora. She knew she was hiding, but she didn't care. No one else knew or cared. He was a murderer. A bigot. And so carefully charming when it mattered. She shivered. She wrapped the scarf through her fingers as she listened to Nora explain the pattern of the towers.

Too soon or not soon enough, the lights flickered and went out. It stayed dark except for the hurricane lamp for thirty heartbeats. When the lights came back on, there was one less sleeper and one less trunk. Iko hurried to rescue the lamp. The next lights out would send it crashing to the ground.

She brought it to sit on the floor near the glittering towers of gold and the glowing greens and oranges. Nora incorporated it into the layout of the city eagerly. As if all she'd been missing was the central fountain or clock tower that the hurricane now reflected. Pam slid her arm around Iko's waist. "Do you want a child some day?"

"I don't know. I wasn't really fond of taking care of my little brother when he was smaller."

"That's different. A child that's yours is different than being forced to take care of someone else's child. Besides, who's happy taking care of a diaper at what? Seven?"

Iko laughed. "At any age, from what I can tell. It's the duty that's done only because it must be, not because we want it to be."

"Is the drunk bothering you?" Pam whispered straight into Iko's ear. Her mouth stayed close, closer than anyone except her mother had ever come. Iko shivered and she couldn't tell if it was because of the question of the delivery.

"He told me about a woman that he says he killed. He told me about a woman he found dead. He's told me stories that I don't want to know and he looks at me as if he wants to eat me alive or rip me to shreds. Yes, he bothers me, but I don't know if there's anything to do about it."

"Let me do your hair," Pam demanded. "I have a brush right here in my bag."

"Okay." There didn't seem to be anything to connect the two topics, but maybe it was merely something else to distract Nora. Iko sat between Pam's legs as the other woman brushed out her hair. She unpinned her hat and set it to the side. Her head felt strange. As if she'd take off some sort of armor that made her invincible. At least she had her gloves on still. They were dirty though, smudged with charcoal and dirt and oil from the seats. There was a drop of blood and a bit of something unidentifiable on her fingers. Lollipop, she remembered suddenly, from Jimmy. Pam coiled the scarf through Iko's hair. And when she was done she decorated it with something sleek and heavy. "Just a 'pick to make your hair more interesting. What do you think, Nora?"

"You look pretty, Miss Maynard."

"Thank you, Nora." Iko shifted her head this way and that to get used to the style. She looked at herself in the mirror of the window. She saw the slender handle that looked more like a decoration than what it was and understood. Pam had given up a piece of her protection. "Thank you, Pam. It's lovely."

She sat back down and crossed her legs under her as if she were a child. The skirt of her dress flowed over her legs and feet, hiding them. She took off her shoes, surprised now at how steady she'd gotten on them, but feeling the relief of not having them. Pam looked at them curiously. "These don't seem to be your style."

"My mother chose them for me. To make me look more adult."

"You need flats."

"First thing when I get to Boston," Iko assured her.

"For now, let's see if we can find an extra pair of sandals in Mrs. Chattergee's things. Even if they're a bit large, they'll still be better for you." They dug through Mrs. Chattergee's suitcases until the unearthed a pair of wooden sandals. Iko slid them on. They fit as if they had been made for her. She also chose a light blue scarf to add to her bag. A remembrance. The sandals felt strange and all the angles of the room seemed subtly changed by the change in height. It didn't matter though, Pam was right. They were better than the heels.

Lewis and Gold came through the front door, looking much more worn than when they'd left. "There is no conductor," Gold said. "Though the train is obviously under someone's control. The settings can't be changed by us. Our hands went through them like the letters."

"There was one sleeper left. But he disappeared during the black out. When we left the luggage car, it disappeared behind us. There was a moment between the car disappearing and us getting into the next car when it wasn't connected to the engine. That's why we're a little windblown."

"We did, however, find a small stash of cheese, crackers and bread." Gold added it to the stash on the chairs. "And we're off for grand adventure and to find the impossible. Another human being."

"Miss Maynard, I love what you've done with your hair." Lewis smiled at her. "And have you gotten smaller or is that my imagination?"

"I'm sure I don't know what you're talking about, sir." She smiled sweetly at him. He shook his head at her.

"Don't fall asleep, Miss Maynard. Whatever you do, don't fall asleep."

"I won't. You'll have a car to come back to."

"Thank you." They went off toward the dining car that might not exist if the crew had managed to clean it up.

"Iko," Pam pulled her to sit between her and Ben, "do you write poetry? Stories? Draw?"

"I danced for awhile as a child. And I can play piano. But I'm not creative."

"Maybe we can teach you that. What do you say? Travel with us for a few weeks?"

"My mother will kill me."

"After surviving this, I think you can survive anything."

Iko laughed. "You are both so remarkable. Sing me something, Ben. Something happy."

"I specialize in sadness."

"Something angry then."

"Angry." He considered for a moment. He started what sounded like a lament and resolved itself into an unanswered call for a missing soldier in a war that wasn't yet and a country that didn't care about the man who hadn't come home. She shivered. It was angry, but it was subtle and slid into her mind like a fierce memory of somewhere else. Anger, hot and heavy coiled in her stomach, but she didn't know where to direct it. She raised a hand to her throat and ghosted along the memory of bruises that didn't exist. Her reflection did the same, except when she looked, she could see the shadow of bruises and the trickle of something viscous and slow running down. It was a trick of the light, she contented herself. A crack of lightening and an explosion of rain battered at the windows.

"Jesus, fuck," Serendinski cursed. He set the empty bottle on the ground. He crossed to sit by the center aisle across from Ben. He studied the towers. "Very impressive." He lifted his eyes to Iko's face. "I love what you've done with your hair. It looks almost traditional."

Chapter 13

"Thank you," she said. There was no call to be rude. She didn't think he'd try anything or say anything uncomfortable while they were in a group like this. Serendinski seemed to be restrained by the presence of other people. He would be perfectly charming and she didn't have to hate him during it.

"Nora, what are you creating?" Pam's voice was sweet.

"A graveyard."

"A graveyard? For what?"

"This is my parents. This is Mrs. Chattergee. This is the general." Nora's voice was sing-song as if she were reciting a nursery rhyme. "And this is me."

"Nora, you're not dying." The little girl looked up with such old eyes that Iko's breath caught. "Nora? What's wrong?"

"I am dying. I have cancer."

"Oh, sweetie." Pam closed her eyes. Even Serendinski looked upset. Iko felt something calm and warm in her chest. Maybe this was just a waiting room. Or a way to get from life to death. Maybe they should all lay down to sleep. Nora set out graves for each of them in simple chunky bracelets surrounding the oil lamp. "And is that one for each of us?"

"Not for Miss Maynard. She won't be in this one."

"Oh?"

Nora shook her head. "She'll be in the special one."

"The special one?" Pam asked.

"For the others."

"What others?"

Nora ignored the question and redid her layout. "I don't like it here. This isn't a fun adventure anymore. Mother said it would be fun."

"After you left the museums?"

"Yes. She said that we'd have fun on the trip to Boston, but I'm not having any fun. Are you?"

"I can't say that I am," Iko replied before Pam could push any further. "Let's see what we can do to make it fun. I can go fetch the cards from Mr. Gold's seat. We can play Go Fish."

Nora looked up at her with her sweet blue eyes. "I'll get them." She popped up from the floor and hurried across to get the cards. The rain whipped in through the open windows.

"We should close those." Pam closed the closest one.

Serendinski didn't move. He simply stared at the small graveyard of bracelets. His face was wan and his eyes seemed barely focused. "Those sandals are probably pretty noisy when they're not on carpet."

Iko's fingers clutched. "Yes, they probably are," she agreed. Don't be rude. Don't provoke him. There's no need to expose Nora to his nastiness.

Nora presented the cards to Iko. "You get to deal." She cleared away the dress-up clothes. She made a neat little bundle as if she were running away from home. Pam smiled at that. They settled it on the seat near the window. Pam sat on the floor under the window, not seeming to care about the wetness there. Nora sat near her, careful to avoid the puddle. Ben chuckled. He set aside his guitar and settled onto the floor with his back to the aisle. He moved the oil lamp between the seats. "Are you two going to join us? It's always a better game with more people."

Iko slid off of the seat and to the ground. She tucked her skirt out of the way. Pam poked at the hem with the toe of her ballet flat. She winked. Serendinski seemed to have a mental debate before he sat down next to Ben. Iko's heart clenched. She'd have to get past him to do anything in the car now. She was trapped. She forced a breath into her lungs and shuffled the cards with awkward hands. She dealt and the game began. It was so easy to lose themselves in a child's pursuit. Anything to change what was happening.

They were on their fifth hand when the door opened. Ben looked over. His face creased in distress. "Mr. Lewis, what's happened?"

"We found... We found the porters."

"You did? Where is Mr. Gold?"

"He's talking with the only one that's awake. They won't be coming to collect our tickets. Ben, tell me there's scotch left." Pam pointed to the seat where the bottle glimmered in the light. The only reason it was still there was that Serendinski was too drunk to stand right now. Lewis poured a generous helping into his mug. He patted his satchel absently as he took his first sip.

"You found something?"

"We did. And the dining car is missing again. There was a snack cart in the third class car. And one sleeper yet to hold the car in place. We stripped it for as much as we could stash in the bag."

"You left Gold behind?"

Lewis closed his eyes. "He, he may not be coming back to join us. Or he may. It all depends on what he finds out from the porters and whether they decide he's too much trouble to let go."

"What's happening here? Did the porters explain things?" Iko wanted to smack him with a newspaper until he got to the point. Lewis simply sipped his scotch.

"We made it through the cars that still exist. There aren't nearly as many as there were when we went to get the oil lamps. We found the snack cart and then pressed on. Gold thought we might be able to find the luggage car or a freight car because there's no reason for those to stay or to go unless they're completely empty from people disappearing. It seemed to make sense.

"We pushed on until we found the luggage car. The poor thing had one piece of luggage left in it. We ransacked it and brought back the pens and paper and books. He wasn't content to stop until we made it to the tail of the train or we were turned back by some staff member, so we kept going.

"The final car we came to, had the staff. They were all sleeping, but not in chairs or like they'd just fallen that way. They were all on bunks, except for one old man who was sitting in his bunk, his eyes fixed on the door. He was the first person who could talk to us. The lights went down in there. I don't know if it happened here. And the rain started. Gold sent me back with our haul." Lewis' hand shook. "He wanted an interview with the man. I just want him to come back already."

He unpacked the satchel. There were snacks and cheese and three bottles of wine that Iko suspected had come from the porter's area. There was also a load of tools. Screwdrivers, pliers, and hammers. He left them all in Serendinski's area and came to watch the game with damaged eyes. He seemed tired and washed out.

Gold stumbled through the door. There was blood on his shirt. "He didn't want me to leave." His voice was thin. Lewis moved to catch him before he collapsed and settled him in the first seat available. He tore open the pink shirt. The tee shirt below it was stained with red the color of the carpet.

"Did he stab you or shoot you?"

"Stabbed me. Took his not-so-little-knife and ran me through."

A little of the life came back into Lewis' face. It was as if having an emergency was something that he could understand. "Miss Maynard, do you have a sewing kit?"

"I think there's one in my trunk." She stood a little unsteadily. She edged past Serendinski, making sure that not even her skirt touched him. She searched through her trunk until she found the small lacquer box of sewing supplies her mother wouldn't let her leave home without. She brought them to him. He'd cut the shirt away.

"Sam. Sam. It's okay. Don't bother so." Gold's smile was strained with pain.

"Don't give me that. You're hurt. Miss Maynard, I need a needle and thread, the hurricane lamp, and some water."

She collected the water in a semi-clean mug. She had a feeling it wouldn't matter soon. Ben had handed over the lamp and Pam was threading the needle for him. She'd also brought over the scotch. Gold bolted down a few mouthfuls. "Thanks, sweetheart." His eyes were closed and there was sweat on his brow, but he was still awake and at this point, that was all they needed from him. Lewis heated the needle and then soaked the thread in a small amount of the scotch.

"Your stitches are awful. I should tell you that." Gold brushed his fingers through Lewis' hair.

"I've seen your mending. At least I know how to do this."

Gold shook his head and clenched his teeth. "I'd say make Nora look away, but I expect it's too late for that. Do you remember that time in Georgia when you cut your arm on the rocks?"

"I had to sew myself up. I remember it very clearly."

"And do you remember when I drowned? We were twenty-one and you'd just lost Martha."

Lewis' hands shook. "Home at the vineyard. We went to the pond and were swimming and acting like children." He forced himself to continue putting in the neat, even stitches. The gash in Gold's side closed together.

"And I took a dive off of the ledge and hit my head. Do you remember?"

"You were in a coma for a month."

"And then what happened?"

Lewis' hands stilled. He looked up until their eyes met. "You died."

"I did." Gold's smile was sad. "And you kept me alive. It's time to let me go."

"No."

"Let me go or come with me."

Lewis closed his eyes and rested his forehead on Gold's knee. The needle was abandoned half-way through the gash. Gold put a hand onto Lewis' head. He faded away, but it wasn't the same. There was no flickering.

There was no sudden disappearance. It was more a sense that there was something missing.

Chapter 14

Lewis rested against the seat. There was no blood on his hands. Iko stared at them. "What just happened?"

"I remembered."

Iko frowned. "What did you remember?"

"That Dom's been dead for years. That I've been keeping his identity alive. I've been filing stories in his name. I've been taking calls and interviews as him for years." Lewis pulled his knees in toward his chest. He looked up at her with a wan smile. "He'd make a horrible husband, Miss Maynard." His voice choked a bit.

He sat on the floor and rested his arm on the chair. The little lacquer sewing kit sat on the floor next to him, cover open and a needle threaded with black thread. He used it to reattach the button that had fallen off of his vest without bothering to remove it. His now pink tie had a small drop of ink on it. Mr. Gold's ring glittered on his hand. A silver pocket-watch chain glittered from his pocket. Iko sat down carefully in the seat next to Ben. Her head felt light.

"What did the porter tell you?" Ben asked.

"They will be serving breakfast from eight until ten thirty. Lunch will being at noon until two. Coffee and tea at three. Dinner from six to nine. And that passengers are not allowed in the staff areas." Lewis' fingers shook. "Our attempts to circumvent the proper nature of things is not appreciated."

"Proper nature of things?" Serendinski echoed.

"They didn't seem to care for the fact that I wasn't using my true name."

"What name were you using then?"

"Gold. Dom Gold instead of Sam Lewis. They didn't like that at all."

"Did they say why they didn't like it?"

"It wasn't the name on my ticket. I don't know why that matters. I don't remember my ticket having a name beyond which station I was going to and a number. Does yours?"

"No. And it wouldn't have Pam in any case. But we just paid for the ticket when we got onto the train." She frowned. "No, that's not right. We had the ticket when we were at the station. The police didn't have any reason to pull us in when we were just waiting for a train."

"You two have been on the train the longest. Was there any hint of anything unusual before the sleeping hit?"

Serendinski looked up. "I've been on since Atlanta. There wasn't any thing strange going on down there. It's been a normal train ride."

"And you get blindingly drunk on the trains."

"Only when I'm going to visit my Ma. She wouldn't know me sober." He let out a bitter laugh. "She's been dead and gone for ten years now. I didn't stay sober at her funeral either. No one really cared then. Everyone in the family was a little drunk. My Pa was so drunk he couldn't stand up."

"I thought you got on in Richmond? To visit your mother" Iko countered. Her eyes narrowed.

"I couldn't remember where I got on. Now I do. I was in Atlanta. I've been out of the Navy for two years. I was in Atlanta learning how to make furniture. Sell furniture? Something like that." His voice trailed off and his eyes unfocussed again. "Clip-clop sandals. You're just doing this to torment me aren't you?"

"I don't know what you mean. These are Mrs. Chattergee's." Iko sat up straight and focussed her eyes on the back of the seat in front of her. She didn't want to see the missing spot where Mr. Gold should have been. She looked down at the graveyard and discovered that one of the bracelets was no longer in place. She bit her lip to keep from asking Nora why that was. No one else seemed to remember Mr. Gold was an actual person anymore. He'd disappeared more completely than even Mrs. Wells and Jimmy.

"Tell me, Mr. Lewis, why didn't you use your name when you talked to them?" Pam's voice was soft. Her eyes were distant again, like she was seeing something the rest of them couldn't.

"I often use Dom Gold when I'm interviewing people. He was a childhood friend and I don't think he'd mind that I use his name when I don't want it traced back to me. I use him as a pen name. The editors at the Times are fine with it. And my agent doesn't think it's a problem that 'Dom' writes my books and I edit them. It keeps people from bothering me. My wife didn't worry about Dom traveling."

"Does she need to worry?" Iko was sure that his wife was dead. Then again, she'd been sure Gold was alive.

Lewis tied off the thread around the stem of the button and bit it to cut it. He carefully stored it away and closed the sewing box. He put the box with the rest of the tools. "Thank you for the use of your kit, Miss Maynard."

"Mr. Lewis," Pam pressed, "does she need to worry?"

"No. Not anymore. She's dead. She's been dead for years. The Germans killed her. She died in my arms. My son died in a hospital bed three days later." He wouldn't meet their eyes. "I'm sorry. I shouldn't have said that in front of Nora."

"It's okay, Mr. Lewis. I know that people die. I'm going to die soon too. It's okay."

"What are you talking about, Nora?"

"She's ill. That's why they were on this trip," Iko answered for her. "This was a trip for fun before she had to take more treatments."

Lewis nodded. "I see." His hands fluttered around him like startled birds. He couldn't seem to lift his eyes from their study of the oil lamp's flame. "And do we know why we're the last ones? Have we discovered some great meaning to all of this?"

"Maybe there isn't any meaning," Serendinski broke in. "There's no reason why this couldn't just be some random madness that's hit us all. There's no reason, just which seats we were sitting. No deeper meaning. Nothing but six people who are stuck in this car with no escape. Maybe the general had the right idea. Maybe all we need to do is off ourselves and we'll be fine and happy in the next life."

"Or maybe we need to find a way out of here." Lewis fiddled with the lamp, making the flame brighter.

"What way out? We can't stop it. You found that out. We can't go to the dining car and threaten the staff. They'll ignore anything that isn't normal behavior." Serendinski's hands gestured widely as he spoke.

"No, no they chastised you at dinner. Maybe there is a way to get through to them. Maybe at breakfast we can ask them directly what's happening. Maybe one of them will answer us."

"And maybe they'll ignore us or try to slash us like they did Mr. Lewis' button."

"Slashed? It just came loose."

"No, it didn't. You told us that a porter took a swing at you with his knife. Isn't that right?"

Lewis frowned. His eyes lifted and they seemed more present again. "Yes, that's right. Why did I forget him being so angry at my being there?"

"It's this train!" Pam's voice spiraled up and echoed. "They are controlling what we see and what we know. They control what we eat and where we go. We need to get off of it."

"How? By throwing ourselves off into the darkness while we're barreling forward?"

"Next time we come near a station, why not? We throw ourselves out into water or onto grass. We just escape."

"Were there any hobos in the freight car?"

"No. There was only one bag in the luggage car."

"The freight car," Ben pressed.

Lewis looked at him, his lips curled down into a frown. He peered into the flame as he thought. "Yes, there was someone there. I don't remember if he was sleeping or not."

"We should go talk to him. Me and Pam I mean. We've jumped a few cars in our time."

"Oh your great time upon this earth." Lewis shook his head. "You're what, almost twenty-five?"

Pam laughed. "That's sweet. I'm thirty-one and Ben's thirty-five. I think we're old enough to make this trip by ourselves. You guys hold the fort."

"I want to come," Nora said.

"No, it's best if you stay here."

"I won't be in the way. I want to stay with you, Miss Pam. Please?"

Pam wavered. "All right. It can't be any more dangerous than staying here." She settled the little girl on her hip, all the little bracelets on Nora's wrist started to jangle.

"Watch my scarves, please, Miss Maynard."

"Of course." Iko folded the first scarf she picked up into a neat little square. Ben slung his guitar across his back and opened the door.

"Wait." Lewis rummaged around in the tools. He uncovered a small green flashlight. "Your flashlight, Pam."

Pam tucked it into her belt. "Off to find an adventure."

Chapter 15

The door closed behind them with a thump, leaving an awkward silence between the last three people in the room. "So, tell me, Mr. Lewis, when did you meet Mr. Gold?" Iko asked.

"We were always the best of friends. I can't even remember when we met. We must have been in school? Seven or eight maybe?" He shook his head. "He was the best man at my wedding and my right hand when we were pulling tricks on people at school. We knew each other inside and out. He was the first to know about the first woman I kissed and I knew about his first time picking locks."

"And then?"

"And then, I went into the resistance and he became a reporter. He traveled the world and sent me reams and reams of letters until I could mimic his handwriting when I sent my letters back to him." Lewis' smile was fond. "And when the war was over and I was all of twenty-one, I was a widower who'd lost his child as well. So he traveled the world and sent back reams of letters and I turned them into articles and columns. And then he died. I lost both of my best friends within a year."

"And what happened then?"

"I traveled. I sent articles to newspapers up and down the coast in Dom's name and we lived happily ever after."

"Until you didn't."

"I survived. And I carried on. And here I am, stuck in a train to nowhere." He leaned his head on the seat. "I'm beginning to think just sleeping might be better than this not knowing. It's driving me crazy."

Serendinski snorted. "I think we were all crazy when we got on the train, just in different ways. Except for Miss Maynard. I think she was sane before we got to her."

"You might be right about that." Lewis offered her a tired smile. "I'm terribly sorry that we may have infected you with our madness. Are you going to run off and become a beat poetess?"

"No, I think I shall become a reporter and write about how the trains never run on time," she replied.

Serendinski looked at her with a smirk. "I think you should do a piece on how women disappear when you least expect it. Or maybe on how the food just isn't good on these long trips."

"Oh, that sounds like a series. Traveling on your stomach. How to lose weight while imbibing rubbery chicken dinners and cheap wine," Lewis said.

Iko giggled. "Or how to maintain a girlish figure when all you want is a chocolate bar and a milkshake?"

"What's your favorite meal, Mr. Serendinski?" Lewis asked.

The sailor leaned back. "Brown bread with fresh butter. While the bread is still warm. Like it just came out of the oven. With strong black coffee and thin sliced ham to accompany it."

"Miss Maynard?"

"Salmon, the way my mother used to make it when I was very young. She'd slice it paper thin and cook it in boiling water and sesame oil. Then, she'd add a little sauce to it and serve it with white rice and sesame balls. I think there was honey or sugar in them. And you, Mr. Lewis?"

"Hot dogs. Very pedestrian of me, I know, but I like good beef hot dogs or handmade sausages with spicy mustard and homemade potato salad with vinegar like my grandmother made. And crispy white rolls that eat up the roof of your mouth when you eat them too quickly."

"I used to eat raw fish when I was in Japan. My girl would feed it to me and I never could tell her no about anything."

"Did you like it?" Iko leaned forward a little bit. "I never could manage to get my mother to explain why Grandmother ate it that way."

"It's okay. But it's got to be fresh enough that it just melts in your mouth. Otherwise it's just weird. Like you forgot to cook it."

Lewis pushed himself off of the floor and took Ben's seat. He looked down at his suit, frowning at the state of his pants. There were small tears at the knees and a drop of oil and coal dust on the corner of his suitcoat. He wiped at it with fingers that were just as dirty. "If you'll excuse me for a moment." He escaped into the bathroom.

"Do you remember meeting Mr. Gold?" Iko asked.

Serendinski looked at her. He cocked his head to the side. "I remember. He was wearing a linen suit. But that can't be true. He isn't here."

"He was here. I'm sure of it. And he's not one of the sleepers."

"No, no, we just heard stories about him. About how he taught Mr. Lewis card tricks, like he was showing Nora. And how he used to make coins appear. What he would do, or what he'd say. He wasn't really here."

"I think he was." Iko reached for Pam's sketchbook, but it wasn't there. She searched the seats around her and turned her eyes to her abandoned seat in the middle of the car. She saw it sitting there, forlornly open to Mrs. Wells and Jimmy. The train shook as she crossed the aisle. She fell, startling a gasp out of herself as she caught herself on the arm of the chair. It didn't hurt. It merely surprised her.

Serendinski was on his feet as soon as he heard her. His hand was at her waist. "Careful," he murmured. "Don't want to bang up your pretty face." She shivered. When she raised her eyes to the window, she could see them reflected there. The smudge of charcoal on her cheek looked like warpaint. He stood a good head taller than she did. His face was casually calm, but she couldn't see his eyes. There was only the darkness and the rain. He ran his hand up her back.

She stepped away. She picked up the sketchbook and returned to her seat. She wasn't going to give him the satisfaction of disconcerting her. She flipped back until she found the picture of the man that Pam saw Mr. Gold to be. "This is what Pam saw him as." She turned the book.

Serendinski looked at it. "That's not the man I keep thinking of. He's too young for one. And his clothes are too casual."

"But are the eyes the same?"

He studied the portrait for a long moment. "Yes. I remember the eyes. Let me see the sketches. Did she do one of me?"

"I asked her to do everyone and you were one of the ones she did after Mr. Gold. There's several of Ben, of course. And I don't think she's done Nora yet." He nodded and he looked through the book. The sound of tearing paper caught her unawares. "What are you doing?" she demanded.

"Taking a memory." He rolled the picture up and tucked it into the pocket of his suitcoat. "This is how she sees me?" He chuckled. "Not a very literal artist is she?"

"No, but I think she's a truthful artist just the same." Lewis returned to his seat. His hands were clean and he'd taken a moment to wet down his hair. Iko could only approve of the changes that made. He looked like a proper gentleman again. If one that was down on his luck. There was nothing for that but a new suit. He crossed his ankles and tucked them up under his seat. "Do you still have your newspaper, Mr. Lewis?"

"Oh, yes. I think I put it in my bag." He fetched it for her with a smile. He picked up the cards scattered in the area while she read the front page of the paper. She spread it out, unwilling to restrain it the way he had. Newsprint smeared onto the tips of her gloves and she didn't care in the least. "Do you play cribbage, Mr. Serendinski?"

"You have a board with you?"

"I travel with it. My wife and I had years long tournaments." He fished around in his bag and came up with a handmade, folding cribbage board. He pulled two markers out of the hidden drawer in the base. For the first time, Serendinski's smile looked genuine. Lewis moved to take the window-seat so that they could use the seat across from Iko to hold the board and the cards.

Iko lost herself in foreign policies and op-eds on civil rights. She read about communists and money and all the small things that she had never bothered to pay attention to. Someone had actually made it to the top of Everest in the Himalayas. Soon she had read up on sports she didn't care about. The Arts section filled her in on movies she would never see and plays she couldn't afford. She didn't listen to the conversation that bantered over the cribbage board. She felt as if she were at home, sitting in front of her father's chair reading for school and doing her homework in spiral bound notebooks and a pen that liked to leak on her fingers.

The door opened. Ben preceded Pam and Nora into the car. "His name is Horace and he refuses to leave his car. He says he's been there since New Orleans and the staff doesn't bother about him."

"Has he ever heard of something like this happening?"

"He hasn't noticed anything strange. We talked about seeing the country and he told us where to find the best handouts at each stop, but there was nothing about sleeping or people disappearing. It was like talking to a recording."

"Like someone stuck in another time," Pam put in. "I don't think he knows anything that can help us. But he did show us where to find the food that isn't in the dining car. And he showed us how to hide when the detectives come through at the stops. He thought Nora was the most adorable train hopper that he'd ever seen. He gave her a little bird he'd carved."

Nora was staring blankly at the world from Pam's shoulder. She gripped her little wooden bird. "I'm tired."

"I know, sweetie. I know." Pam patted the girl's back. "Why don't you show Miss Maynard your new bird." Pam neatened up the newspapers so that Nora could sit next to Iko. Ben settled near the window and Pam settled on his lap, with her arms around his neck.

"I've named him Terry." Nora held out the wooden sparrow. The little wings were cut in and his eyes seemed almost real. There was even a hint of individual feathers here and there.

"He's lovely. I especially like his wings."

"He looks like the little bird that likes to sit outside of my window when I'm at the hospital. He looks at me with black eyes and occasionally he'll even say something. But mostly he just sits there and doesn't do anything but watch me. He doesn't even get scared away by the nurses."

"Do you think you'd like to work as a nurse?"

"No. They have to touch too much icky stuff. And I don't think it's very nice what the doctors do to them. They're mean to them and they don't even apologize when they make one of them cry. The little hats seem so uncomfortable too."

"Hats don't have to be uncomfortable. You get used to them." Iko looked around for her hat. It was sitting abandoned next to Mr. Lewis' seat. She fetched it and placed it on Nora's head. It was just a bit too big for her. The little girl laughed though.

"Does it match my scarf?"

"It does. It looks lovely."

Nora yawned wide, showing one missing tooth. One looked to be loose as well. She blinked her watering eyes. "I can't stay awake anymore, Miss Maynard," she whispered. "Don't let Miss Pam cry. It's okay."

Iko unraveled one pigtail. She combed it out with her fingers letting it cascade in small waves. By the time she'd undone the other one, the young girl was asleep. She slumped over in the chair, leaning her head on the arm. Iko shook her gently. "Wake up, Nora," she said firmly. The little girl grumbled in her sleep and turned over. "Wake up."

The sweet blue eyes opened briefly. "I'm tired." Her voice slurred. She went back to sleep. Iko blinked back tears. She lifted Nora up and sat down with her on her lap. The gentle breathing made and steady heartbeat weren't comforting. She looked at Pam.

The artist looked back, biting her lip. "I won't cry," she said finally. "I won't cry because she doesn't want me to cry."

"That's my girl," Ben said. He kissed Pam's mouth gently. Iko stared. Of all the things today, that was probably the most shocking. Even her parents didn't kiss in front of her. Pam kissed him back, holding him to her as if he were going to slip away. Iko politely averted her eyes. Lewis and Serendinski were studiously avoiding the situation.

"Nasty weather we're having," Lewis said. There was a wry twist to his lips.

"Yes, just awful. All sound and fury and it's nearly impossible to hear oneself think," Iko responded.

Serendinski snorted. "Or we can talk about the loose behavior. It doesn't bother me. Does two people kissing bother you, Miss Maynard?"

"It is not something I have a lot of experience in, Mr. Serendinski."

"I would have though that a girl like you had men beating down the doors to get to her."

"A girl like me?"

"Sweet. Pretty. Unmarried."

"Perhaps I am not interested in the men who would beat down the doors to get to me. Perhaps I am only interested in those who treat me kindly and distantly." She tugged at the stubborn ponytail holder. Nora didn't even seem to notice. She didn't even try to turn her head.

"It's not nice to tease, Miss Maynard. What would your mother say?"

"Why on earth are you talking to two men to whom you were not introduced? Only she would be yelling it and scolding me with a finger." She'd also be telling Iko to be silent because a woman should not be loud. She should never challenge a man's opinions. Mother had never met Mr. Serendinski.

"And my mother would be chiding me for talking to a young woman who was traveling without a chaperone," Lewis murmured.

"I am old enough to look after myself, Mr. Lewis."

"I don't doubt it. My mother took exception to unmarried women traveling. Though, by all accounts she did a fair amount of traveling herself when she was in the younger world."

"My Ma would scream herself hoarse if my sister decided to get a job outside of Boston where she could keep an eye on her."

"Tell me about your sister?"

Serendinski smiled to himself. "She was younger than me. A couple of years younger. And I used to frighten off her boyfriends. She was killed on Halloween. There was a prank and they thought she was someone else, someone who could get out of the room they locked her in. Took us two days and a lot of threats to find her."

"Oh, that's horrible."

"Yeah, it was. So was her face when we found her. She was terrified when she died. It was pitch black and she was afraid of the dark. The doctor said her heart was weak. And it just gave out. I've always thought they did something more than just lock her in." His smile turned to a frown. "Why do we always start talking about death when you ask me a question?"

"I don't know, Mr. Serendinski." Iko closed her eyes and breathed in the warm vanilla and baby powder scent of Nora.

# Cherry Blossom Express

Chapter 16

No one spoke for a long time. The wind buffeted the car, lashing rain onto the windowpanes. Lewis and Serendinski's card game continued unabated. Ben and Pam were curled together like kittens. Pam laid her head on Ben's shoulder and he hummed softly in her ear, some sweet Spanish melody that Iko had heard somewhere before. She rocked Nora without thinking about it. Her mind spun away into memories of home. She remembered the sound of soldiers as they came to the front door and told her mother to pack one bag each because they were being moved to a camp. Her little brother hadn't even understood what that meant. He thought they were going to see Daddy. She remembered staring at the flag in the front window that showed her father was off at war as they were driven out of the area.

She remembered the smell of horses and dirt in the converted stables they were living in at the camp. She remembered her mother stifling her tears until the dead of night because it was unbecoming to cry in front of anyone. Iko had taken that lesson to heart. Even when she'd broken up with Sean in high school she hadn't cried in front of anyone.

They'd moved from California as soon as her father had gotten back to town and rescued them from the camps. At least that's how it had felt at the time. She remembered the soft Virginia summer and reading in the welcoming arms of a tree that didn't care about her eyes or the color of her mother's skin. She remembered walking in the swirl of cherry blossoms as her mother told her a story of when the government had held hands out in friendship, not war to Japan. She remembered the rush of what she thought was true love when boyfriend had held her hand for the first time. The memories were distant now, as though they belonged to someone else. Iko shook her head and came back to the present.

Nora snuffled in her sleep, moving a little this way and that. She murmured low about horses and tack and her little nose wrinkled up as if she'd smelled something unpleasant. Iko rocked her, glad to hear her voice, small though it was. She didn't think she'd be able to stand it if someone else disappeared right now. The world outside felt like a dark blanket thrown over a bird's cage. She tried to keep herself focussed on the smell of Nora's hair, the snick of the cards and the soft humming that Ben didn't seem capable of controlling.

Eventually, the sound of the water drove her to put Nora on the seat and escape to the bathroom. She let her spine curve with exhaustion as she braced herself on the sink. She washed her hands and her face. She did her best to scrub off the charcoal marks with her fingertips. She didn't think it was going to work. She worked at the line of charcoal that ran across the front of her neck. She contemplated washing her skirt, but water on silk would probably exacerbate the problem.

She pulled her gloves on as she left the bathroom. She crossed to look in on Mrs. Chattergee and the general. "They're gone!" she cried out.

That brought Lewis to his feet. He was in the luggage room in an instant. There was no trace of the dead bodies that had been there. No trace that they'd even existed. "Mr. Serendinski, check the luggage."

"Right." Serendinski poked his nose around the luggage area. "It's looking a little empty. There's one trunk left, two dufflebags, and one camel colored suitcase."

"Sadly that makes sense. Is our stash still available?"

"Yes," Iko reported back from the seats. "The oil lamps are gone. The ones that were in the hatbox."

"Damn it. Pardon my language, ladies. We haven't lost power though."

"No, but we've never needed to lose power to lose people," Ben reminded them.

"Is the train moving faster?" Pam's voice was shaky. "It feels like we're gaining speed."

"There's no reason to think we aren't," Lewis said.

"Let's break out the wine," Serendinski said. "I don't know about you, but I don't feel like traveling at breakneck speed sober."

"I second that motion," Ben said. He pulled a hand-rolled cigarette from his pocket. "I'll share."

"I'll definitely take you up on that offer." Lewis smiled wryly. "And Miss Maynard, would you like a drink of something harder than tea?"

"At this point, Mr. Lewis, I think I am more than willing to consider trying Ben's cigarette as well."

"We'll make a beat-girl of you yet," Pam laughed. "Come sit by me and I'll show you the technique." The lights went out right about then. The little oil lamp struggled valiantly, but couldn't do more than cast a warm glow around the edge of the seats. There was an arm around her waist and a broad hand on her hip.

"This way, Miss Maynard." It wasn't Lewis' arm. She forced herself not to react badly to Serendinski's touch. She let him escort her back to her seat. Pam's hand reached out of the darkness to settled on her shoulder.

"Mr. Lewis." Ben held out the lit cigarette. It smouldered orange in the lack of light. It was brighter than the carpet. It flared brighter as Lewis inhaled. The strangeness of the smoke made her nose wrinkle up and her eyes narrow. It was sharp and bitter and nothing like what she thought of as tobacco.

Lewis passed it to Pam who offered it to Iko. "On second thought. I think I will stick to wine."

"A fine choice," Lewis informed her. He poured her a generous mug of wine and handed it across the space. She sipped at it while the four around her proceeded to relax and slip into loose jokes and banter. The sound of Nora breathing and muttering in her sleep made her shoulders relax. She stroked the little girl's back. "Tell me, Miss Maynard, do you like this wine?" Lewis asked.

"It is not as good as what we had at lunch, but it is better than the wine at dinner."

"That is true. I am not a great wine drinker myself, so I have very little to compare it to. Do you drink wine often, Mr. Serendinski?"

"I prefer hard spirits, myself. I think we'll find the wine tastes better if we smoke more and faster."

"I agree," Ben said. He raised his mug with the cigarette between his fingers. He took a deep inhalation off of it and passed it on to Pam. Iko could only see the edges of the people around her. Nora was reduced to glimmering gold hair and a blue dress. Pam was a white cuff with black smeared on it. Ben was a white mug and cigarette. Mr. Lewis was shining pearl buttons on the edge of his cuff and a card in his hand. Serendinski was shimmering, ragged fingernails. The wine bottle glinted in the soft like, illuminated stained glass with no label she could see.

The little sparrow that rested amidst the glittering circles of Nora's graveyard seemed alive. His eyes, made of pinheads shone in the darkling light like a real creatures. He regarded her with intelligence. Smoke swirled around the car, caught by the closed windows and the wall. It danced in and out of the light like a gypsy skirt. Iko blinked rapidly. She was almost asleep. She swore she could remember the sparrow moving.

Nora turned over in her sleep and Iko's heart jumped for joy. She was still alive and more than that, she wasn't in the same type of sleep as the Sleepers. She would still awake to their prodding if she reached over right now. Lewis was flipping a coin through his fingers and it sent spinning reflections around the room. They danced over Ben's face and hands. They decorated Pam's still face. She'd finally succumbed to sleep.

Iko turned her head, feeling slow and clumsy. Ben was awake, but there were tears running down his face. He was writing in frantic twitches on a piece of paper from the little notebook she had seen him contemplating earlier in the day. She didn't know if he was writing a song or a poem or if he was simply writing a letter to his future self or the person who might find them at the end of this journey.

Serendinski had a knife out and was cleaning his nails with it. The catch of light on the silver blade made her think of ripples on a pond. She forced herself to bring Gold's face into her mind. She concentrated on painting him in her memory and moved on to Mrs. Chattergee. Then, she thought of the general and his flopping mustache. They were happy in their death, she knew. Gold had been dead and lingering as part of Lewis' mind for a very long time. It was probably best for him to sleep as well. "The dead do not sleep," she murmured. "Isn't there a poem like that Ben?"

"Shakespeare, maybe. Or maybe the Bible. I was never a good Sunday school boy. I thought it was Death does not sleep though, rather than the dead. To sleep perchance to dream. In death what dreams may come? Something like that. Hamlet maybe? Do you know, Mr. Lewis?"

"Not off hand. It's something I'd look up to fact check before I wrote it down somewhere. Do you think we're all dreaming?"

"No, no, if we were dreaming then we wouldn't be interacting like this would we. We'd be slaying dragons or be stuck inside of dancing flowers or talking to the animals. The only person talking to animals here is Nora."

"There's nothing wrong with talking to the animals," Serendinski said with a smirk. "I think it's admirable to treat those who are less than we are with respect."

"Somehow I think you're lying through your teeth," Ben told him. "In fact, I think you learned that line specifically to keep yourself out of trouble with someone. Who was it? Your girlfriend or your superior officer?"

"My Commander. He thought that he should talk to the niggers with the same amount of respect he used for the rest of us."

"Once you're in a fight, the enemy doesn't care about the color of your skin."

"Thank you, Mr. Lewis, for that piece of bullshit. Maybe they didn't care in Europe, but they did care elsewhere."

"Only in the States. They don't care in England."

"But they do. Didn't you notice how the general talked about Mrs. Chattergee? She was exotic and foreign and that's why he wanted her. He wouldn't have wanted a white woman, even if she was his mate. He wanted her because she was different. The enemy is no different." Serendinski pointed with the tip of his knife.

"That's where you're wrong. The bullets from a machine gun don't care who they hit." Lewis' voice was hard.

"And no one cares if a white man kills a nigger woman. They only care if it's the other way around. It's the way the world works. No one cares if a Jap girl dies as long as it doesn't happen on base."

"Was the woman you killed Japanese then?" Iko asked. Her tongue felt like it was working without her input. "Or are you talking about Yukio and how no one cared because she was killed by a Japanese man?"

"They've all been Japanese."

"How many women, Mr. Serendinski?"

"Five. Just the five. They all deserved it. They were taunting me and teasing me and pretending to be my Yukio. In the end they were nothing but dime-store whores. You're not a dime-store whore are you, Miss Maynard?"

Chapter 17

Iko held herself stiffly. "I am not a whore of any variety, Mr. Serendinski and you should now that by now. I insist that you stop drinking. You are tolerable sober." She tried to sound like her grandmother Maynard, but she wasn't sure she'd accomplished it. For all she knew she sounded drunk and sloppy like the rest of the conversation. The smoke was making her cough a little bit now. It was heavy and Pam had done her best to blow it into Iko's face. Maybe it was her way of letting her try the cigarette without actually having to put it to her lips. It wasn't helping her feel more solid.

"I think that you are. I think that all it'll take to get you into a bed is a word and a little money here. Maybe dinner if you're too good for actual cash. Don't be so high and mighty. You're not a lady. You're just the byproduct of a whore your father couldn't avoid."

"You should watch your mouth, Mr. Serendinski. I have no qualms about sending you off to the corner like the child you're acting like." Lewis' voice was stern.

"I haven't heard children talking about whores. Your son must have been advanced for his age."

Lewis' teeth showed in the light for a moment. "The wine has made you too relaxed. I think you need to dry out for a little bit. In fact, I think you should probably sleep it off."

"Oh, so now you want me to sleep? That's a laugh. I won't be sleeping until I drop to the floor. I am not just going to go away. I'm not a figment of your imagination. I want Miss Maynard to answer me. Are you a good whore?" Lewis stiffened at that. He looked to be about to speak, but Iko shook her head slowly. She needed to deal with this alone. "Are you going to pretend to be my Yukio and lead me along until you let me know you're lying and unable to manage the simplest of tasks? Are you going to make little rice balls and pretend to put sweet nothings on them in soy sauce? Are you going to pour the sake until we're drunk and let me drink it off the hollow of you collarbone?"

"I am not Yukio. I am not your girlfriend. And, Mr. Serendinski, I will not be your girlfriend or your whore. I would never have dated you in the first place. You're in the Navy and my father would never allow such a thing."

"Your father. Hiding behind your father. How completely typical."

"My father would have to approve our dating. He is in the Army."

That made Ben laugh as though it were the funniest thing he'd heard in ages. Perhaps it was. There'd been few enough opportunities for laughter. Pam woke and stretched.

"I think we should change the subject." Pam tried to keep her voice light. "I think we should talk about our favorite books, or movies, or drinks even. If I have my choice, I'll drink absinthe by the gallon-full as long as there's sugar for it."

"Miss Maynard and I aren't done with this topic."

"Yes, we are," she replied. "I think my favorite is the tea my mother would make me when I was ill. It had enough honey and lemon in it to be more like syrup than tea."

"Oh, southern sweet tea. My favorite. If the spoon doesn't stand up in it, it needs more sugar. My grandmother made it every summer." Ben chuckled at either the thought of tea or the memory. "And I like coffee with chicory which no one really makes outside of Louisiana. And Mr. Lewis?"

"I like beer. Pretty much every beer I've tried throughout the country and the world. There's something so friendly about it."

"Vodka. Good old fashioned potato vodka. My grandfather used to have a still. I think he started it in the thirties and no one bothered to tell him that Prohibition is over, so he keeps making it. That or he likes it better than anything he can get in the stores," Serendinski said.

"My grandfather used to make wine, but I never liked it." Pam's voice was steadier now. "I remember visiting his winery once and he had made me wine without any alcohol in it. It was something his family in Germany had always done for the kids. I still don't like it, but I would drink a bottle of it tomorrow if I had it in my hands. Just because he was the one who made it for me."

"My grandmother used to bake these little cakes to go with tea in the afternoon," Lewis said. His voice was dreamy. "They had creamy fillings and thick frosting. They were the best little pastries I'd ever eaten. Maybe because I could only get them when we were visiting."

"Roulades. My grandmother made roulades when we were coming over and for every holiday. Little rolls of pastry and nuts and jam. They were the best thing about visiting when I was little." Serendinski seemed properly distracted and Iko breathed a sigh of relief. She didn't want him dead. But she didn't trust him.

"There were these beignets my mom would make on Sunday mornings. They were fresh out of the oil and dunked in powdered sugar. They were the best thing on a winter morning. She always served them with black coffee. That's the only way I can drink the stuff. Even though it was especially sharp and bitter to me as a kid. My dad drank it black."

"So did mine. Though sometimes he'd put in a pinch of salt," Iko told him.

"Oh, I learned the salt thing from a soldier. It actually does make a difference," Lewis added. "My father refused to drink anything but tea or wine. Though I've always suspected that he put something more than just sugar syrup in his tea."

"Something that tastes a little more like whiskey?" Serendinski laughed. "Yeah. I understand that. I wouldn't bother with the tea myself. Just the whiskey and a little sweetener and some carbonated water. Mint in the summer."

"Something crisp and cold. I used to chew mint. I'd take it right off of the plant and pop it into my mouth." Ben said.

"Tomatoes. Especially those little tomatoes that grow on the bushes. I could eat a gross of those and still have room for more." Pam sounded steady and awake now.

"Grapes," Iko admitted. "I found a weakness for grapes when I was about fourteen. I think I ate two pounds of them by myself. I was sick for a day after, but it was worth it."

Pam laughed. "I did that with chocolate cake. I made the chocolate cake, frosted it, and ate the whole thing by myself. I can't even argue that I was drunk. I was fifteen and I made it for Home Ec. I didn't like my partners or anyone in my school enough to share."

"Do you remember the tomato soup devil's food cake?"

"I do. And putting that soup into my Mac and Cheese. Oh, I was so sick of smelling it by the end of the rationing."

"I hear they're still rationing in England."

"Oh, those poor bastards," Serendinski said. "Sugar rations."

"And gas rations."

"And cloth rations," Pam added in distress. "Makes me glad to be here. Even if here is a train barreling into the dark and not making any sense to anyone."

Iko smiled, though she was sure no one could see it. "Are you going to marry him? If we manage to get away from this?"

"No, we've been together long enough. And I don't care about someone else saying we're married. We love each other and that's all that matters."

"Love. What crap. What does love profit any of us? All you get from love is tears and a reputation as a dreamer," Serendinski said.

"But there's also the rush of love. The enjoyment of being with someone else. It's worth the pain to feel that joy," Pam told him.

Iko looked over at Nora. Did she want a husband, a child? She didn't know. "When did you write your first song, Ben?"

"Lovely jump in the conversation, Iko," he teased. "I must have been ten the first time. My hands barely fit around the guitar, but I'd been learning it from my father and the old men around the neighborhood when I had a chance. And it seemed so much more real than anything I was learning in school. I didn't bother finishing school after I started playing regular gigs. I met Pam at a jazz club."

"I was singing and doing portraits for a dollar on the street corners to entertain tourists. It worked well enough. I was making enough to live on and he was happy enough to stay in the clubs. We started dating. Then we started crashing together wherever we could find a place. We must have walked the entire state before we decided to take the train and start over somewhere else."

"Just like that?"

"Just like that. There was no one after us for rent. No angry parent looking out for Pam's virtue. Just us and the world to explore and we wanted that. We both wanted out of New Orleans. We were thinking of going to New York at first, but then, the train ended in Boston and we decided that was good enough."

"New York's scene is growing," Lewis commented. "I haven't heard about Boston much. If you want to be at the front of something, Boston's a better bet. New York and you'll just be following the crowd."

Pam laughed. "You are a closet beat aren't you?"

"Not at all. I just travel and people tell me things. People tell me a lot of things, actually. Where to get the best drinks in a city. Where to find a good cup of coffee or the best pie. They also tell me about those kids or their mother's idea of what is right and proper. I sometimes do magic shows when I don't want people to realize that I'm being a reporter and nosing into their news."

"You should do a show for us. When the lights come back on."

"Did they turn the lights out for the overnight trip or do you think the storm caused the problem?" Serendinski said.

"I don't know. Ben?"

"They do it sometimes. So that people can sleep. They might be doing that for this trip. I don't know. It's possible that the storm put them out. Or they're punishing us for trying to interrupt whatever's happening."

"That there's actually a plan, you mean? That's rather frightening to contemplate." Pam's voice was soft. "But on the other hand, a plan would indicate that there's a reason for this. That there's a reason we're chosen to stay awake. That there's a reason for any of this."

"There is a reason. I'm sure there is." Iko spoke quietly. "I don't know what it is. I don't know who's in control. But I know there's a reason. Something is happening here that we'd be able to understand if we just had a little more information. Nora is sleeping normally. She's reacting. She's dreaming. The others weren't. The dead have disappeared. We don't know if they went like the others or just faded away once we'd shut the door on them. I know that their luggage was still there for a little while because Pam and I were using it."

"You believe that Nora will wake up?"

"I do, Pam."

"Then I'll be brave. But I'm not going to sleep. Not fully. I may close my eyes though."

"I won't do that. If I close my eyes, who knows were I'll wake up." Serendinski's voice was sharp.

Iko's eyes drifted shut. "I don't know if I have any choice in the matter."

Chapter 18

She was falling through the air like she was diving. She woke with a jolt and a bruise on her upper arm from where Pam's fingers were digging into the muscle. "No sleeping until we're sure that Nora wakes up." Iko turned her head to regard the sleeping child. She'd curled up on herself and was whimpering.

"Should we wake her up now? I can't tell if she's having a nightmare or not," Iko whispered.

"No, give her a little more time." Iko sat back, but Pam's hand didn't move. Iko bit her lip, but she didn't really want to tell the woman to let go. Being connected to someone right now, pain or not was worth it. "I'd take the chance if I could. No more than five minutes for us. Not until we're sure."

"It's okay. I get it." Iko stroked the back of her hand until Pam released her grip. "I won't fall asleep again. We'll give Nora another hour or two, then wake her up. Okay?"

"Yeah. Yeah. That'll be okay." Pam rested her chin on Ben's shoulder. He stroked her hair. He pulled out the band that was holding it up until it fell free over her shoulders. He massaged the back of her neck with his fingertips. Iko wanted that. She wanted someone who would hold her when she was scared, laugh with her when she was happy, and dry her tears. She wanted someone who'd yell at a police officer. She wanted someone to sing her love songs, share her grief, and treat her like the center of his world.

She turned her eyes to the guttering of the oil lamp. She knelt down next to it, her skirt covering the circles of graves. She turned the wick up so that the flame burned a little brighter. She wanted to see more than the edge of a cuff, the glint of a smile, and the flip of a coin; she wanted to see faces and read body language. She wanted. She wanted everything.

"Miss Maynard, were you dreaming?"

"I was falling."

Lewis didn't say anything about that. She settled herself back in her seat and smoothed down her skirt. She traced the smudges into patterns. "I'll make an artist out of you. Just give me time," Pam murmured. "Why don't you try drawing something yourself?"

"I'm no good at drawing. I'm really not. My art teacher told me to—"

"Screw your art teacher. If you don't practice how will you ever learn to draw? You can't learn anything if you don't practice. You can't write, you can't draw, you can't live if you don't practice. Just pick up my sketchbook and a crayon and draw. Draw like Nora. Just let what's in your head out on the page. Draw like Ben, with words."

"Words. Maybe I can do that."

Lewis had his newspaper and was folding it back into its neat sections. He picked up the red crayon from the floor. He marked out a passage and rearranged another. He'd fallen into editing, she realized. Just to keep himself occupied. Iko picked up the sketchbook that Nora had been using. She opened it to a clear page. She took out Lewis' gold pen and started to write. Everything she could remember from the day. Everything she'd dreamt or wished for. In tiny fine script that would make her teacher tear up in joy, she chronicled the day.

Pam whispered softly into Ben's ear. Iko politely didn't listen. She felt eyes on her and looked up. Serendinski was staring at her. She couldn't see his eyes, but she could feel them crawling on her like ants. He swirled the wine in his cup. "Do you do calligraphy?" His voice was light, but she was instantly alert.

"Yes."

"Yukio said it was the mark of a lady. That if she could write well, she could do other things well. She didn't believe me when I told her that writing in Japanese was calligraphy no matter how sloppy it looked to her."

"It's an artform. I never learned Japanese. I've only ever written in English. And I learned my calligraphy from an old French lady who lived down the street and gave lessons to supplement her income." Iko wasn't sure if he would be disappointed or relieved by that knowledge, but she was surprised to find out that she did care. Why she cared she couldn't say. Perhaps it was knowing that he wouldn't mistake her for someone else again. Or maybe it was just to remind him, once again that she wasn't one of the women he'd seduced.

Pam ran a gentle finger around the curl of Iko's ear. The touch made her shiver. Pam tugged a few strands of hair out of the tight hairstyle that she'd created on the younger woman and curled it around her finger. She used spit to make it curl. Iko shook her head. "Are you bored?"

"Not at all. I have things to see. This light makes interesting shadows."

"I suppose it does," Iko agreed reluctantly. "Are you done with my hair?"

"Not at all." Pam's fingers pulled lightly on the curl to see if it would stay or maybe to watch the shadows change in the half-light. Iko stayed still, keeping her back straight. She continued to write, long spirals of dreams coiling up and back and around.

Nora woke with a sharp cry. She burst into tears. "It hurts, Miss Pam. It hurts!" She wrapped her arms around her middle. Pam gathered her up and walked up and down the aisle rocking her and stroking her hair as she cried.

"Give her some wine. It may help."

"She's too young."

"Pam." Lewis handed her a mug of wine. "You could give her some of your stash to chew on if it isn't mixed with tobacco."

"No." Pam shook her head. "I have something better. I just don't know how much to give her."

"Well, what dose are you supposed to be taking?" Lewis cocked his head to the side.

"One pill every four hours."

"We can crush it up and give her an eighth to start. If that doesn't touch it, we can slowly increase the dose until she's not in pain any longer."

"I'll get them. They're in the duffle right?" Ben asked.

Pam nodded. He stood up. He pressed a kiss to Nora's forehead as he passed. Nora had thankfully stopped asking for her mother. She mumbled complaints into Pam's shoulder. "Mr. Lewis, do you have a penknife we can use to cut the pill?"

"Yes. I'll clean it." He went to the bathroom and came back with a silver penknife. He heated it over the oil-lamp. "There. I don't know what it was used for last, but it should be clean now." Ben handed him a white pill.

"Did one of the men you tossed earlier have a bill clip?"

"Yes. I think it's over there. Dom wouldn't have gotten rid of it." Lewis froze. "I wouldn't have," he corrected. "It's just that I've been used to thinking of him as a different person for so long."

Iko didn't push him. If he were mourning Gold they'd lose his focus. It wasn't as if anyone else remembered him anyway. He busied himself with cutting the pill, grinding it really, to get it small enough. "Miss Maynard, will you get a cup of water for Nora?"

"I have some cold tea left," Pam offered. "It's where Mrs. Chattergee was sitting." Iko found that. It would be better to disguise the taste. She mixed the pill dust into the tea. "Here, Nora. Drink this down. It should make you feel better."

Nora made a face, but drank down the dregs of the tea and the powder. Lewis folded a piece of newsprint up to secure the rest of the powder. He tucked it into his inside pocket. "When we need it, please remind me where I've put it."

Iko nodded. "Of course, Mr. Lewis." Nora whimpered softly into Pam's shoulder. Pam stroked her hair. She'd make an excellent mother some day. Nora calmed a bit.

"Better, sweetheart?"

"Better." Her eyes closed.

"Well, I suppose this means it's safe to sleep." Lewis took a seat in one of the darker areas. "Wake me in an hour, Miss Maynard?"

She glanced at her watch. It was nearly eleven at night. "I will." She sat down with the sketchbook and returned to her work. She made a flower out of her memory of Mrs. Chattergee. The general became a walrus. What to make Mr. Gold. She considered for a long moment before making him a gun. Pam sat Nora back down in her seat. Her eyes were at half-mast already. She stroked the hair away from the young girl's face. She looked sheepishly at Iko.

"I know she's not mine, but she feels like it right now."

"She called for you. She trusts you." Iko put a hand on her wrist. "We'll work it out."

Pam nodded. She picked up her satchel looking for something to entertain Nora. She found an album of some sort. She stroked the side of the page as she stared at it. "My mother was a flapper in the twenties. She had so many pictures of herself. When she started yelling about my seeing my first boyfriend, my father handed me this album. I've kept it ever since to remind myself that there's no reason to be ashamed of what I've done. She was a wild child and there's no reason for me to settle down and be a housewife. She hated it. She hated cleaning the house and mending the linens. When she could work out of the house she was happier than I had ever seen her. I was so happy for her that I wanted to know why she had ever given it up. She tried to explain it, but I wasn't ready to listen to her. I was so angry."

"You can tell her different when we get out of this."

"She's not talking to me anymore. I haven't talked to her since they threw me out of the house."

"You can write her a letter. You never know what she's thinking. She might miss you."

"You can't know that."

"You can't know that she doesn't," Iko challenged.

Pam gave her a half smile. "I'll keep it as an idea."

Ben snorted. "I'll remind you."

"I'm sure you will. Maybe you'll give me something interesting in exchange."

"Maybe." Ben smirked.

"I like your thinking. Sing me something."

"I will as soon as I finish writing it."

Pam laughed at him. "Work faster then. I'm bored."

"Draw me something as inspiration."

Pam picked up her sketchbook. She flipped through it. She frowned at it. "I thought." She shook her head. "Nevermind." She picked up her charcoal stick to draw. She lost herself in the drawing. Iko looked at her watch. It wasn't time yet to wake up Lewis. She wanted to have him there because she didn't want to be alone with Serendinski. Ben just wasn't as comforting a presence.

"Tell me, Miss Maynard, how is the calligraphy coming?"

"It's going well. Thank you for asking. Have you found something to read? There were some journals and magazines on the seats over there."

"I have all I need." Serendinski leaned back casually in his seat and sipped at the newly filled mug of wine.

Her hand trembled as he kept his eyes on her. She took a breath and held it until her hand was under control. It didn't matter if he watched. He couldn't hurt her with his eyes.

Chapter 19

"Mr. Lewis, it's time to wake up." Iko placed a hand on his shoulder. He jerked awake.  He blinked a few times.

"Thank you, Miss Maynard. Shall I look over your sleep?"

"No, thank you. I am not as tired as I was a few hours ago. I can only assume that the power of the wine has faded."

He joined the main group. He looked at Nora in concern. She was sleeping more deeply this time. Her breathing was steady. "Part of me thinks that we should wake her every hour, but the rest of me is rather reluctant to disturb her."

"Let her be." Pam's voice was unexpected. "I think I need to sleep. I can't seem to keep my lines straight. Will you watch over me?"

"I will," Lewis promised. Pam retreated to the far corner and laid down between the seats with a scarf bundled under her head. "Would you like my coat?" he offered.

"No, I'm warm enough. Thank you." The rocking motion of the train and the exhaustion of the day seemed to draw her down between one breath and the next. She was asleep by the time that Lewis had seated himself with his editing.

"What are you working on?" Serendinski asked looking over.

"To be honest, I'm simply marking up the work of journalists I can't stand."

"And there seem to be a lot of them."

"There are very few that I do. For the most part they're drunken louts. And the ones who aren't drunk, are the most useless men I've ever met."

Serendinski laughed. "Sounds like most of the men I know in general."

"I wouldn't be shocked. There are more drunks than sober people from what I can tell."

"Have you ever killed someone, Mr. Lewis?"

"I don't think we should discuss that in front of Miss Maynard."

"Oh, she's used to my conversations. Don't worry. Just answer the question."

"Yes. I have."

"Purposefully?"

"Yes. I knew what I was doing. It was during the war."

"The enemy then. That's not what I meant. Have you killed anyone since you returned to the states?"

"Yes, I have."

"Was it in cold blood or the heat of the moment?"

"I made a choice to kill him." Lewis looked down at his hands, stained with ink. It was as if he could see evidence of what he'd done there. "He'd killed a woman."

"Did you know her?"

"Yes. I knew her. She was my wife's friend. My friend."

"What about you, Miss Maynard. Have you ever killed?"

"No." She spoke quietly.

"And Ben? Surely you have?"

"No. I haven't killed."

"Why not? What stopped you? What do you have that we're missing?"

"Enough passion to do it. I'm a quiet person."

"Would you do something if someone hurt Pam?"

Ben shrugged. "I'll have to wait until it happens to find out." He fingered his guitar and started playing gentle. Ben started to sing with his music. A soft love song that mourned the death of something and didn't explain. Iko felt her eyes pricking. She closed them to listen and was lost to her dreams an instant later.

"Wake up, Miss Maynard," Lewis called as he gently shook her shoulder.

"I'm awake. Thank you."

"Nora is restless. Pam is still sleeping. Do you think you could walk with her a bit more? My shoulder is not comfortable enough for her to rest on. My own son had the same complaint."

"I will." She stood up and wavered. "How long was I asleep?" Her head felt stuffed with cotton and her eyes burned.

"No more than an hour. I didn't think I should wake you without cause, but I didn't dare let you sleep too long.

Ben decided that Pam should continue to sleep. We'll get her up in another hour."

Iko nodded. She picked up Nora and carried her through the car. She walked in even paces. "Are you in pain, Nora?"

"I'm always in pain, but it's not bad." Nora set her head down on Iko's shoulder. "You smell pretty."

"Thank you, sweetheart."

"Miss Pam is nice, but she smells bitter. You smell sweet."

"I think it might be the pain killers that she needs right now."

"Like I need to take pills all the time. I don't like them. They make me feel strange in my head."

"They do that to everyone. It's not just you. But the pain is gone."

"It's never gone. That's the problem that they can't fix. We don't go to the hospital much anymore. I don't have to stay there. They let me stay at home and take medicine there. Mommy gives it to me in needles sometimes and sometimes she sneaks it into my juice. I can always taste it though."

"And do you mind having to take it or that we don't have juice to hide it in?"

Nora shrugged. She managed to curl her hands into Iko's dress and held on. Her little fingers didn't hold on to much, but it tightened the neckline just a bit. "Do you think Miss Pam will weave a scarf into my hair?"

"We can ask her when she wakes up. What color scarf do you want?"

"Purple. It will match my dress nicely, I think. Do you think maybe she could put one of the bracelets into it?"

"I think that would be very possible. It will give us something to do until breakfast is served. What do you like for breakfast?"

"Oatmeal with brown sugar and raisins. Or bacon that's very crispy. I don't get to have that much anymore. It makes me sick to my stomach."

"And what is your favorite food?"

"Chocolate cake with white frosting and little colored sprinkles. That's what I have on my birthday. What do you have on your birthday?"

"I have white cake with chocolate frosting. My mother makes little roses to put on top. One for every year of my age."

"And when is your birthday?"

"April. Around the time that the cherries blossom."

"Mine is near Halloween. Every year I get to dress up as something different. Mommy wanted me to be a princess this year, but I told her that I wanted to be a frog. She tried not to laugh, but she painted my face bright green and she made me a little dress and got me green tights. I got to eat a whole popcorn ball by myself."

"My mother likes to hang rice paper lanterns on my birthday. She says it reminds her of what Grandmother used to do for the first days of spring. It was like having fairy lights dancing in the air. I remember last Halloween. My little brother decided he was going to be a wolfman."

Nora giggled. "My Daddy dressed up like a gentleman and took Mommy to a dance. I got to stay with Grandma and Grandpa. Grandpa lets me stay up late."

"That's nice of him. Did you make it very late?"

"I fell asleep on his lap when he was reading me one of his stories. He likes stories about rocket ships. I think they're boring."

"Oh, why? Don't you want to see if the moon is made of green cheese?"

Nora shook her head. "No. It can't be made of cheese. It would have gone bad by now."

"Maybe it's different in space. Maybe green cheese can last longer in space than it does down here."

"Maybe." Nora frowned. She obviously wasn't buying the idea. "When will Miss Pam be waking up?"

Iko looked at the little silver watch. "In a little while. She was tired."

"I'm still tired."

"I know. You can go back to sleep."

Nora shook her head. "I have bad dreams."

"What do you dream?"

"That Mommy is calling for me and can't find me, even though I'm right in front of her. That the pain in my bones is getting worse. That someone's hurting Daddy. He's crying. Daddy never cries. And of the nurses poking me with needles. I don't like needles."

"I don't like needles much either."

"Will you play Go Fish?"

"Yes." Iko set Nora down and held her shoulders until she was steady in the rocking car. They settled between the men's legs, in the glow of the light, to play with the little cards. There was a tear on the corner of the King of Hearts, but she didn't mention it. If they were playing poker, it would be different. If they were playing poker, Iko's mother would be pulling her away and chiding her that it was a man's game and she should have nothing to do with it. Her father would take her on his knee and teach her how to read the hands. She smiled as she dealt the cards. Her father would despair to see her wasting the lessons he'd taught like this.

"Deal me in," Serendinski said. He didn't sit on the floor. Iko looked up, suddenly wary, but he seemed genuinely bored. She dealt him a hand and they played. Ben fiddled through a song that sounded classical. He had added flourishes to it though, so she couldn't be sure.

"What are you playing, Ben?"

"Variations on a theme I heard once. I haven't gotten it quite right yet. I think there's more hiding between the notes that I haven't gotten to embellish. And I'm still playing with the words for it." He changed to a more recognizable tune.

"I know that one!" Nora said.

"Twinkle, twinkle little bat."

"No! No! It's star," Nora corrected.

"Of course, my mistake." Ben laughed gently. He went on to repeat the simple tune, adding more and more trills and cords until it was practically unrecognizable. Iko smiled at the sound. There were those in her family who would discount Ben as a talentless hobo, but he wasn't any less of an artist then the men that played on the records. "Tell me, sister, do you hear the wind?" he murmured. "It's calling your name tonight."

Iko shivered. "Mr. Lewis, is it time to rouse Pam?"

Lewis consulted his pocket-watch "Yes, it is." He picked his way through the card game, steadying himself on the back of Serendinski's seat for a moment. There was a hard gust of wind that rocked the car. He seemed shaken by it. He knelt down by Pam. He called her name softly, then with a bit more urgency. "Pam!" he said sharply. "Pam. Wake. Up."

"Five more minutes," she mumbled.

"No, Pam. Up you get. It will be time for coffee and morning pastries soon enough. If there are no pastries at least we have cheese and crackers. The wine, I'm afraid has run out."

"Getting me up and not having any wine. That's downright uncharitable."

Lewis laughed softly. "Miss Nora requests that you use your artistry to weave her a purple crown."

Pam stood. She seemed like a storybook ghost for a moment. All Iko could see was her white shirt glowing in the light. When she sat down behind Nora, her face seemed ashen. As if she were in too much pain to not show it. "I think I should take one of those pills myself." Ben handed her one and the bottle of absinthe. Pam took a shot of the powerful alcohol and swallowed her pill. "Now, Nora, I hear you want purple. It's the color of kings and queens you know."

"And I shall be a princess."

"Yes, you'll be our princess."

Iko handed up a simple gold bracelet. "Perhaps you could make this a part of her crown."

"Yes, I think I can manage that. Ben, hand me my brush please."

Nora sat still, eyes closed as she leaned against Pam's leg. Pam teased her hair up into a high braid and ran the scarf through it, securing the bracelet at the front of Nora's forehead with a rubber band and a little twist of braids.

"Iko, do you have a hair pin?" Iko discovered her purse under one of the chairs and pulled one out. It glittered as the interior lights came on to bath them all with sharp light that cast unfamiliar shadows over them all.

Chapter 20

Iko handed Pam the bobby-pin. She fixed it in the back of Nora's hair to secure her braids there. "There."

"You look like a proper princess," Lewis said. He gave her a formal bow. "My Lady Nora, would you do me the honor of this dance?" Nora giggled. "Ben, if you would?"

"Yes, sir!" Ben laughed. He played a darling little waltz. Lewis carefully escorted Nora in small circles in the aisle. She stood on his feet and he carried her along. His smile was bright. He deposited her back at the start and Ben finished up the melody.

"Thank you."

Nora did a very credible curtsey. She curled up on Pam's lap. Pam leaned her head against the side of the seat and closed her eyes. There were pain lines etched around her mouth now. Iko put a hand on her ankle and squeezed in silent support. She cleaned up the card game and blew out the lamp to conserve the oil.

Serendinski offered his hand as she got to her feet. She gave him a polite smile. "Thank you. I'm fine." She cleared away the detritus of the evening's entertainment. Her little silver watch told her that it was six in the morning. They had two hours to fill before breakfast. She could, perhaps, take a nap. "Mr. Lewis, if you would be so kind as to watch the time for me?"

"Of course, Miss Maynard." She laid down, with her skirt toward the windows. It wasn't that she thought Serendinski would try something in the light, she just didn't want to make herself any more of a target. She closed her eyes and let the train rock her into sleep. Her sleep was dream filled. She heard the screeching of an owl in the distance as she woke in a tangled wood of black trees and snow. She wandered through the woodlands, looking for the path in the little areas that were starting to melt through.

She saw small round stepping stones and followed them down the path to what looked like a small house made of the paper screens her mother had used to divide the play room and living room in their small house. She entered, very aware of the damage on her dress and the oddness of her hair.

The woman there smiled up. Her deep brown skin was marked with blue paint and she wore a white dress. "Sit down, Little Sister. I will make the tea."

"Thank you, Sister." She sat down on the indicated cushion and let her skirt cover her crossed legs. She looked down at her gloveless hands and thought of her mother's horror. Her fingernail on the left hand was bleeding. She must have been chewing on it without realizing. There was nothing to be done, but ignore it.

The little old lady returned with tea and two cups. "You will see the sunrise," she stated. "But tonight the wind calls your name and there are wolves in the trees."

"Sister?" Iko's eyes widened.

"Drink your tea. Eat your sweet cakes. There is time enough for worry after the tea is done." She poured the tea into the small blue cups. "Do you not recognize me, Iko?"

She stared. A double image seemed to snap into place. "Mrs. Chattergee?" The woman laughed. It was the caw of a raven and the call of an owl and the dust of the heat and warmth of the morning sun. "That is the name you knew me by. Now, I will go to a new life and so shall you."

"Miss Maynard. Miss Maynard, it is time to wake up."

Iko opened her eyes. For a moment all she could see was dove grey fabric and a very distinct charcoal stain. She could smell copper and oil this close. "You've cut yourself."

"It's stopped bleeding. I tripped on the car that wasn't there." Lewis said wryly. He let her get to her feet by herself. "We're about to head to breakfast, in hopes of answers." He dropped his voice. "Pam's not well. She doesn't want to come with us, but if she doesn't go, then Nora won't go."

"I'll support her, if you can carry Nora. And Ben?"

"He's frantic, but trying to not show it. He's been scribbling in his notebook for the better part of two hours. He barely even looks up if it isn't to look at Pam."

"He was writing her a love song." Iko shrugged her shoulders. "Perhaps he thinks it will make her push through her pain a little bit, if he gives her something new."

"Perhaps. If you're ready?"

Iko left her purse and hat behind. "Walk with me, Pam," she ordered gently. She offered her arm and the other woman managed a small laugh and smile. She curled her arm around Iko's shoulders. Iko wrapped her arm around Pam's waist, startled by how fragile she felt. This was how Ben could stand to keep her on his lap for hours, then. Nora was curled up on Lewis' shoulder. Serendinski gestured Ben ahead and brought up the rear.

That did not make Iko's nerves feel any better, but there was no choice in the matter. Pam needed the help and Ben, Ben needed someone to guide his steps while he continued to write.

The dining car was so bright and cheerful that Iko felt that she should shade her eyes. The tablecloths were white and filled with crystal and silver. There were sharp red flowers in crystal bud vases. The white expanse made her feel grubby and insecure. She glanced down at her ruined pink silk and snagged stockings. She forced herself to move forward and settle Pam at the first table. Pam pressed a hand to her side. The waiter moved in with a dazzling smile and soft brown eyes.

"Breakfast?"

Pam managed a tight smile. "Some toast and tea please. Dry toast."

"Of course, Ma'am. Shall I bring a menu?" He smiled at Nora and reached out to tug gently on the braid. Nora smiled up at him, turning her face to the side.

"Please." Ben settled next to Pam and Iko took the seat next to Nora. She'd need to help the girl with her breakfast. Across the aisle in the seats nearest to the window, Serendinski and Lewis sat. They requested menus and black coffee. Ben looked out the window. "The rain's stopped."

"The streets look wet still." Pam's voice was tight with pain.

"Where are the people?" Nora's voice was soft.

"They might still be asleep," Ben offered.

"Like Mommy and Daddy?"

"Just like that."

The waiter returned with menus and juice for the tables. "We have fresh brown bread. The cooks just finished baking it," he informed Serendinski.

The sailor looked up, startled. "Brown bread with butter. And cinnamon and sugar if you have it."

"Of course, sir."

"I'll have eggs over easy and hash." Lewis informed him.

He took the orders from around Iko's table and disappeared into the back room. Iko sipped from her water glass. She looked at the window, hoping to catch her reflection. All she could see was her hair, dark and neatly sculpted, and her eyes, dark and rimmed with sleeplessness. The dark line that had been lingering around her throat seemed to have disappeared. Perhaps the quick rinse she'd done in the bathroom had actually gotten rid of the graphite.

Pam closed her eyes and leaned her head against the window. "Wake me when the food gets here, please."

Ben put his arm around her and pulled her until her head rested on his shoulder. He rested his head on her cheek and closed his eyes. He hid a yawn with his hand. "I should have taken a nap last night." He gave Iko a wan smile. "I think I've nearly got my song finished though."

"I would love to hear it when we return to the car."

Nora played with the silverware. "Miss Maynard? I'm not feeling so good."

"Is the pain back, sweetheart?" The little girl nodded. Her hair shone in the morning light like gold. "Mr. Lewis, did you bring Nora's medication?" Lewis patted his jacket pockets. He produced the newsprint of powder and handed it across the aisle. Iko contemplated the powder. She poured it out onto the bread plate. It wouldn't hurt her if she got a little into her system. "Do you think it's safe to increase the dosage?"

Lewis nodded. "The last dose didn't last long. Perhaps a quarter of what's left?"

Iko nodded acknowledgement of that. She parceled it out and scraped it into Nora's juice. She stirred it with the silver knife. The crystal chimed like a bell. "Here. Drink this down."

Nora held the glass with both hands. She drank it with long, greedy sips. She held out the empty glass. Iko ignored the residue at the bottom of the glass and set it aside. "Ben, did Pam miss a dose?"

"She hasn't taken it regularly. I think being tired just made things worse. I wouldn't worry about her." Ben didn't smile. He toyed with his smallest fork. "Why do they put out so many pieces of silverware when they know we won't use them in the morning?"

"Tradition?" Iko shrugged. "I've never taken an overnight train like this before. I've only ever done small trips or trips with my family. My father prefers to drive. I'm beginning to be more sympathetic to that idea. Despite the fact that my little brother still enjoys playing demented versions of I Spy."

Ben chuckled. "My mother was always the one complaining on car trips. They didn't agree with her stomach. She had this yellow scarf she'd wear whenever we went on a trip. It was egg yolk yellow and it made her look greener than she actually was."

Nora giggled. Her eyes were drooping. "Mommy wears black these days. She says she thinks it makes her look thinner. I think she just likes wearing black because it makes the people at church think she's a teacher."

Iko ran her hand down Nora's back, soothing her until the little girl curled up against her side. Her skin felt cool to the touch. Iko looked over at Lewis, but he was deep in conversation with Serendinski. She didn't know what they'd found to discuss, but it was full of acronyms and numbers. Probably some sort of sports.

"Iko." Ben's voice made her turn her head sharply. "I just wanted to say, thank you. You gave Pam something to do earlier and that made all the difference. I really appreciate it."

Chapter 21

Pam sat down heavily in her seat in the corner of the car. She seemed relieved to be back in the familiar space. Her head lolled to the side and rested on the window. She stared out at the passing country-side. Iko settled Nora next to her. The little girl was asleep from the drugs now. Ben watched Pam sleeping. He'd picked up his guitar and was randomly picking out tunes. He didn't seem to be thinking anything at all. Iko settled down next to him.

Serendinski sat beside her and she repressed the automatic shiver that threatened to make her hands shake. Lewis handed her the film section of the paper and she shook her head. "No, thank you, Mr. Lewis. I have pen and paper." She settled back in her seat just a bit. She didn't know if she were trying to prove to herself or someone else that she was relaxed. She continued writing everything she could remember from Lewis and Gold's interrogations, from her discussions with every passenger. Even the discussions with Serendinski.

"Don't write that. I didn't kill her."

"I didn't say that you did." Iko jumped as Serendinski's hand crumpled the page and tore it from the newspaper. She slid into Ben's arm. The songwriter looked over. His eyes were unfocussed. He blinked rapidly.

"Watch yourself," he hissed at Serendinski. "Are you okay?"

"I'm fine. He just startled me."

Serendinski snorted. He stalked away from the little group to hide in the bathroom. He slammed the door shut after himself.

Lewis looked up from his newspaper. "Would you like me to switch seats?"

"No. It's fine. He won't do anything."

"Are you certain?"

She nodded. Lewis looked as if he wanted to argue with her, but he didn't open his mouth. He folded his paper with sharp movements, like an angry teacher. He looked over at Nora. His gaze moved beyond her gently moving chest and he froze, eyes widening. Iko followed his line of sight. Pam's head lolled to the side and her hands lay motionless in her lap.

"Pam. Pam, wake up." Ben moved slowly. He sank to his knees in front of her. He picked up her hand. "Pam. Pam, my beauty, wake up."

Iko stepped across the car. Her skin looked like chalk this close. She took Pam's other hand in hers and checked for a pulse. She pressed two fingers to her throat. There was nothing. The artist's arm was limp under her fingers. She set it down gently. She lifted one eyelid and saw nothing but wide pupils like a cat at night. Iko grimaced. She held her hand under Pam's nose.

"Ben." She shook the songwriter's shoulder. He was babbling out something to the woman. He didn't react to her touch.

Lewis caught Iko's arm before she could shake him out of his panic. "No, let him finish. Let him tell her the song before you make him face facts."

She caught a spark of grief in Lewis' face. She nodded. She went to the luggage compartment, to make sure that it was still clear. There were no traces of Mrs. Chattergee or the general there. She wiped at her eyes. She was not going to cry where someone could hear her. Tears battered at the back of her eyes and filled her sinuses. She pushed them down with deep breaths. The door opened and her head turned automatically.

Serendinski's hand closed over her mouth, shoving her against the wall as the door closed behind him. She pulled at his wrist, trying to get his fingers away from her nose, so she could at least breathe, if not yell out.

"Stay quiet," he hissed at her.

His breath smelled of alcohol and her eyes widened. She hadn't seen him get any from the waiter, but then, she'd been distracted, carrying Nora and helping settle her. Maybe he'd found the opportunity then. His breath was sour and sharp. She could even smell it on his skin.

"You've been teasing me this whole trip. With your eyes and your smile. Flirting with all of the men. Flirting with that whore and her boyfriend." Iko strained to shake her head against the painful grip that held her face. She tried to pull in air and smelled the tang of sweat and dirt. He eased off slightly as her head began to swim and her eyes lost focus. "And then you had her do up your hair like the geisha you are."

He pulled the rolled up picture from the inside of his coat. He shook it at her face. It was wrinkled and smudged but the cherry-blossoms and the Arizona toothpick were still visible. "She drew you like the Jap whore you are. And I am not going to take this treatment anymore. Do you understand me?" The words echoed in her ears, repeated from somewhere else. Someone else?

Serendinski threw Iko to the floor. It was hard and uncarpeted – .cold and slightly damp, as though someone had just cleaned it. She hit with a grunt of pain. The impact shot up her arms to her shoulders. She turned over and kicked out as he tried for her. She drew in gasps of breath as he came back. She hoped suddenly that the others had heard him hit the wall. "Mr. Lewis! Ben!" She cried out, hoping for safety or help or maybe just to have a witness.

He sneered at her. "Your johns are busy with a dead body." He blocked the door handle with a broom from the corner. It should be a mop, she thought wildly, though she didn't know why. "There. Now we won't be disturbed."

She scrabbled to get to her feet, but he knocked them out from under her. The rocking of the train worked against her. She rolled under the lower shelf, curling up and hooking her feet around the support the way she'd hidden under her bed when the Army came to take her family out of their home. Her head hit the wall as she flinched away from his hand. The solid thunk against the wall made her eyes widen. It wasn't her skull.

She grabbed the knife that Pam had woven into her hair. She wrapped shaking fingers around the hilt. The grip was solid in her hand, smooth and warm from her own body heat. She jabbed at Serendinski's hand when he reached for her. "Lewis! Ben!" she called out. "Gold!" she tried in desperation. Anyone, even Nora.

There were sounds at the door and the broom shook in its position, but didn't give way. Serendinski dove for her, dragging her out by the belt at her waist. She thrust at his chest with desperation and the blade bounced off. He yelped in pain.

"You goddamned bitch!"

He grabbed for her wrist and the knife, but she stabbed at his arm this time. Blood flowed from the wound as she pulled out. He pulled back for just an instant. She thrust once more at his chest as he lunged forward. The blade went through his throat and a shower of crimson splattered her face and her hands. She let go of the knife.

He collapsed across her and she could hear the whining of his breath and see his eyes widen in terror. He grabbed at the knife, rolling off of her in his panic. She made it to the door and pulled the broom out of the way. The door burst open, and Lewis caught her as she wavered.

She clung to his lapels and breathed in the warm smell of him. "Are you alright, Miss Maynard?"

She shook her head. She saw blood smears on his shirt and released his suit. He didn't move his arms.

"Are you hurt?"

"No. Not my blood," she managed. She couldn't seem to breathe. Lewis ran a soothing hand over her back.

He set her down in Serendinski's first seat and went to investigate the damage in the luggage room. She turned her head and saw that Pam had been laid out between the seats where Mrs. Chattergee had fallen. Her hands were laid over her chest. Ben was laying next to her. One of his arms was wrapped around her waist. He seemed to be asleep. His breathing was regular and his eyes closed. His guitar was strapped to his back.

For one desperate moment, it looked as if his breathing had stopped. "No," Iko whispered. She stumbled across the car to check on him. He was still breathing, but his breath was rapid and shallow as if he were running or having a nightmare. She debated waking him when Mr. Lewis emerged from the luggage compartment. He was wiping off the knife with a handkerchief. He gave her a paternal smile, as if she'd just done something to be proud of.

Her face remained blank.

He set the knife under Pam's hands where a rose should have gone. "I have the rest of her medication. We can use it for Nora or ourselves, should it come to that." Cold-blooded man.

"I'm going to wash up." Iko escaped to the bathroom locking the door behind her. She threw up twice before she managed to stumble to the washbowl. She scrubbed at the blood on her hands and her face. The water was a soft pink. It finally ran clear and she kept scrubbing. She could still feel it on her face.

She looked into the mirror. What she saw there was a clean if over-rubbed face. She put the towel down and stared for a long moment. She should look different. There should be more difference than wet, stray hairs curling around her face wet from washing. There were bruises forming on her cheeks and throat that looked like fingerprints.

She sobbed once, then pushed the tears back down. She couldn't cry. Not right now. Maybe when she was truly alone and there was no one to hear her. She dabbed at the blood on the bodice of her dress. She sucked in a breath.

"Mr. Lewis," she called out. Her voice was steadier than she had any right to expect.

"Yes, Miss Maynard."

The voice was far too close to the door and she reared back. "Would you be so kind as to fetch a clean dress from my trunk? I seem to have spilled something on this one."

"Of course."

She took deep even breaths and told herself that the smell of copper was her imagination. There was nothing on her dress. She wiped at the tears that ran down her cheeks. How dare they disobey her. There was a polite knock on the door.

He handed in a dress of pale yellow with pink stripes on the bodice. Of course he would pick the one that matched his own taste. "Thank you, Mr. Lewis." She closed the door firmly once more and stripped out of her dress.

She let the ruined silk sit on the floor. She washed her chest and across her abdomen, anywhere he'd touched. There were bruises on her hips and bruises on her ankles. She discarded her ruined stockings in the trash bin. She put on the yellow dress. She smoothed it over her body and did up the tiny buttons. She slipped on the wooden sandals. She left her hair alone. Let Pam's work unravel as slowly as it wanted. She took a deep breath and held it. Then, she opened the door.

Mr. Lewis was carefully grinding up pills. "I brought some juice from the dining car. The waiters were more than accommodating. We won't have to put them in water."

"Very good." She sat down at her seat and picked up the little gold pen and her notebook. She took down some notes, but abandoned the project. She tucked the pen away behind her ear in the absent way she thought she'd trained herself out of in high school. She didn't bother to correct herself. "How is she?" Better than the dead man in the luggage room, her conscience told her.

"She's sleeping peacefully. She was talking in her sleep about a pony. I think that's a good sign?"

Iko nodded. "It sounds like a good sign to me. Is Ben?"

"Ben is... Ben was hurt too," he said after a moment's thought. "He took a toke and put himself to sleep. I don't know. I don't want to wake him if it doesn't seem desperate."

"He seemed to be having a nightmare."

"I can't tell if it's a nightmare or just drugs. It's a fine line."

"I see."

"Miss Maynard, forgive me, but are you sure you're alright? He didn't hurt you?"

She met his eyes, tipping her chin up in defiance. "I'm a little bruised. A little scared still. But I will be fine." Her fingers clenched the cotton of her skirt.

"If anything I do disturbs you, please tell me." He leaned forward a bit. His eyes were earnest. "Shall I discard your dress?"

She shivered. "Yes. Please. Shove it as deep into the trash as you can manage. I don't want to see it again."

He nodded. "I'm going to take this opportunity to change my shirt." He gave her a small smile. "And my trousers if they haven't manged to be irreparably wrinkled by their time in my case." He pulled out a clean pair of pants and a pale yellow shirt. He fingered a blue tie for a long moment, but put it back. Iko's eyes lingered on his movements. She was aware of every step and movement that he made.

Nora snuffled in her sleep. She whimpered. Iko knelt beside her and stroked a hand over her hair. The little gold bracelet shone as the sun glinted off of the carvings. Curled up she looked like a little fairy in her flower. She was crying in her sleep. Iko wiped away the tears with gentle fingers. She looked at her bitten nails and the traces of brownish red that lingered in the cuticles. She stood up and found her trunk.

She stared at the neatly folded clothes from a lifetime ago. She traced a finger over the hat nestled in the corner and the neatly coiled belt underneath it. She didn't remember why she had ever liked it in the first place. The little flowers were too coy and the lace a little too sweet. She picked up her pink gloves and pulled them on. They covered the little knicks and the new bruises and the small traces of blood. Her hands shook as she opened the small jewelry box. She pulled out the small silver necklace with its single pearl on the end and fastened it around her neck.

She stood as the bathroom door opened. Her skirt swirled around her legs as she spun. Lewis froze. He held his hands out to the side. He was carrying nothing but a white undershirt. "Miss Maynard, do you want my penknife?"

She shook her head. "No. No, I'm alright."

"Can I offer a game of cribbage?"

"Yes, thank you." Iko's voice was shaky.

Chapter 22

Nora woke up and rubbed her eyes. "Miss Pam?"

Iko's breath caught. "Sorry, sweetie. Miss Pam isn't... she can't..."

Lewis' eyes darted to hers, wide and panicked.

Nora looked at Iko with wide blue eyes. "Did Miss Pam die?"

"Yes, sweetheart," Lewis confirmed. The little girl sniffled. She buried her face in Lewis' shoulder. He kissed the top of her head. She cried unabashedly.

"I want Mommy."

"I'm sorry, sweetie." He turned so that she could crawl into his lap. He set his hand of cards down on her seat. She sobbed into the side of his neck. He patted her back. He looked for his handkerchief with the other hand. Iko set down her cards and moved to her trunk once more. She fetched him a clean cotton handkerchief with a sweet kitten on it. It was soft and worn – edged in purple. He nodded in thanks. He used it to clean Nora's face as she calmed down. She blew her nose less than delicately. She crumpled the cloth in her little fist.

"Do you want some lunch?"

Iko swallowed. "Yes, that's probably the best idea. Shall we wake Ben up?"

"No, let him sleep."

She narrowed her eyes at him. "Is there something I should know?"

He dropped his eyes to the side.

"And no using Nora as an excuse."

"Ben doesn't want to wake up. He just wants to be with her. For a little bit longer."

Nora's eyes grew wide. "Will he disappear? Like Mommy?"

Lewis looked up at her with pleading eyes. Iko took pity on him. "We don't know." Nora was quiet then.

Lewis led the way to the dining car with Nora in his arms. Iko was still surprised that it appeared as they opened the door. The tablecloths were yellow this time. "Three of the special of the day please."

"Of course, sir."

They settled Nora in the chair near the window. She stared out at the farms on the country-side. She toyed with the cloth in her hands. The waiter brought a small doll made out of a napkin for her. She gave him a watery smile. "Thank you."

Iko and Lewis discussed nothing of importance. Nora poked at the food on her plate. Sweetly flavored rice and lightly breaded chicken. Iko felt her hair slip down the back of her neck. The sweet rice stuck in her throat. She coughed discretely. Lewis' head snapped up. His smile was a bit brittle. "Are you alright?"

"I'm fine. Thanks."

"Miss Maynard?"

"Yes, Nora?"

"I want to sleep. Like Mr. Ben and Mommy."

Iko bit her lip. She took a deep breath. "Of course. Mr. Lewis?"

"We'll take some more juice with us."

Nora played with her little doll, feeding her pieces of rice and sliced apple. It was like being a family for a moment. Lewis looked down at his plate. Iko took a shaky breath. She looked out at the passing farmland. It looked like a series of landscapes from a cartoon. The uninhabited towns looked something from a play. "Mr. Lewis, can you identify the state we're in?"

He looked out the window. His eyes were suspiciously wet. "It looks like Vermont."

"Well, I've never been there." Iko crumpled the napkin in her lap.

"Would you like some dessert?" the waiter asked.

"Yes, please." Nora gave him a sweet smile.

He smiled back at her, his teeth bright against his skin. "We have chocolate cake?"

"With white frosting?"

"Yes, Missy. White frosting and jimmies."

Nora bounced in her seat.

"For the lady and gentleman, I suggest the rice pudding or the lemon meringue pie."

"I'll take the lemon," Iko said.

"Me as well. And could we get some juice and some tea to take to the car with us?"

"Of course, sir. We'll pack up some small snacks?"

"That would be kind. Thank you."

The conversation stayed rather stilted. Iko picked at her lemon pie. It was sharp and sweet. It made her think of her mother in the kitchen with fresh lemons and a grater. "I used to whip the eggs for my mother. My father loves lemon pie."

"My friend Dom used to love rice pudding. Ben and I were discussing it. He likes it with raisins. I was always more partial to almonds."

"I don't think I've ever had it."

"Nora, would you like to taste the lemon pie?"

"No, thank you."

The waiter brought them a silver tray with the rice pudding, cheese, bread, tea, coffee, and juice. Iko sipped at her water with lemon. She drew patterns in the meringue that was left on her plate with her fork. Nora hugged her new little doll to her chest. The small smile that had been on her face had faded. Iko raised her eyes. Lewis looked at her evenly. He drank down the last of his water.

"Are you ready to go back to the car, Nora?"

She nodded.

"Do you want me or Miss Maynard to carry you?"

"I want to walk."

"I'll take the tray, then," Iko said. She stood, then dropped her crumpled napkin onto the table. There was a yellow stain across the side of it. She lifted the tray as she would have picked up her grandmother's tea service. Lewis helped Nora over the gap between the cars, then held the doors for Iko. Lewis pressed Nora's head to her shoulder so that she wouldn't look into the luggage area.

Iko set the tray down on the floor. She glanced at the luggage area. She didn't see any obvious changes there. Serendinski lay where he'd fallen. Blood splattered the wall and seeped across the floor. Lewis powdered the pills. Iko stepped carefully into the sleeping area. Ben was there, curled up as if Pam's body were still there. He was awake. His eyes were screwed shut as if to block out reality. There were tears on his cheeks. She put a hand on his arm. "Ben, we brought you some rice pudding and some coffee."

"She's gone." His voice was a small, broken thing. "I didn't think it could hurt anymore than it already did, but I was wrong, so wrong. Don't fall in love, Iko." He rubbed at his face and eyes with his sleeve. "Don't listen to stupid love songs. We're all liars. All lovers are liars."

"Ben." She couldn't think of anything else to say. There was nothing to make it better. "Come eat something."

"Mr. Ben, come sit next to me?" Nora's voice was crisp, like bells in the air.

The musician took one deep breath, then another. "Of course," he managed after a minute of ragged breathing. He pulled himself to his feet. Iko stepped into his space and pressed a daring hug to his waist. "Thank you," he whispered. He settled into his seat.

Lewis gave him a half-smile. He handed him one of the black coffees. He continued to stir until two full pills were in the juice. Iko bit her lips. "Is that too much?"

"A quarter pill doesn't help the pain. And half doesn't even make her sleep." He shrugged. His eyes looked desperate. The pills were dissolved soon enough. Nora put her hands out for it and drank it down quickly. A little trickle of orange juice ran down her chin. Iko wiped it up with a clean hankie from her trunk.

Ben looked between them. He cocked his head to the side in question. "She wants to sleep like her parents," Iko answered.

Nora patted Ben's knee. "Will you sing me a lullaby, Mr. Ben?"

"Sure."

She curled up in the seat and leaned her head against him as he put his arm around her. He sang softly until her eyes slipped shut and her breath evened out. He looked at Lewis. "You have any of those pills left?"

"Yes. There should be," his voice broke. "There should be enough if you want to take a nap."

Ben looked out at the sun soaked fields. "Not yet. I have something to finish up. But if I change my mind?"

"I'll keep them right here."

Chapter 23

Iko plucked at the wrist band of her gloves. There was a little lace there and it was starting to irritate her skin. She contemplated taking them off. It wasn't as if the men hadn't already seen her ragged nails. She peeled off one and then the other. She tucked them into her purse. Ben was writing quietly in his notebook.

Lewis was busy editing and rearranging the paper to his satisfaction. He'd folded to the crossword and was busy changing the clues. She didn't know if he were making it harder or easier. She picked up the sketchbook and started on another pattern of words. She wanted to remember Nora, in case—no, for when—she was whisked away from them. She created a little castle for her and her memories of cake and walking back and forth as if she were Iko's own child. She made a little hospital bed of Nora and Pam's interactions and the pretty braid in her hair.

She continued until Lewis cleared his throat. "Miss Maynard, do you play cribbage?"

"I have." She wrinkled her brow in confusion. Hadn't they been playing when Nora woke up? A little twinkle in his eyes made her realize the joke. She narrowed her eyes at him.

"Would you like to play?"

She felt a pale reflection of a smile lift up the corners of her mouth. "Yes. I think I would like a game." She set the book aside. "Shall I move over to give us more room?"

He nodded. She moved to the seat near the window. Ben didn't look up from his work. He shoveled in spoonfuls of rice pudding. The silver spoon clinked against the side of the dish with syncopated rhythm. She couldn't tell if it were on purpose or not. Lewis dealt the first hand and she soon lost herself in the game. The little blue and red pegs moved slowly up the scorecard toward the finish line.

Ben started to croon snatches of melody. It was an aimless, mournful weaving of sound that wound around them just under the sound of the wheels. Nora snuffled in her sleep, whether from dreams or pain didn't matter. The sound drew all of their attention to her.

"She's still asleep," Lewis said softly. "And only asleep. God have mercy on our souls."

"Hope it's deep enough that she'll see her mother soon," Ben murmured. "I know we couldn't leave her there, but it just seems wrong to think that she'd never see her again."

"In time, I hope we all see those who mean the most to us." Lewis looked down at his hand of cards. "I believe you may beat me yet, Miss Maynard."

She laughed at that. "Maybe."

"Iko, do you want any of Pam's things? They should be in my bag."

"I don't know."

"Why don't I show you? I'd rather you have them than some stranger who never knew her and wouldn't understand what she was like. I think they'll fit."

They wedged themselves into the luggage area. Iko opened the top of her trunk and reverently laid Pam's sketchbook in the top. She wasn't giving up those pictures. Ben dumped his duffle bag across the seats. Iko felt her cheeks heat as his underthings spilled out. It was different than seeing her father's or her brother's when she did the wash. Ben laughed at her. It was a surprising sound. "Don't worry. I don't think Pam will mind if you look at my boxers. Pam wouldn't mind if you looked at all of my things." He smirked. "I wouldn't mind either."

"Benjamin! Be nice to Miss Maynard," Lewis called back.

"I will not. She's an adult. She can tell me off if I upset her."

"You are not upsetting me. I have a brother remember? I know more than my father would like to believe."

"Your brother's what? Sixteen?"

"Fourteen. He's my little brother." Iko shook her head. "He's trouble. A real rebel in a sweater-vest and tie."

"Sweater-vests can be very subversive." Ben rolled his eyes. "So, what does he want to be when he grows up?"

"I think he's leaning towards being a mathematician."

"And what do you dream of being?"

Iko shifted the little gold pen from hand to hand. "I haven't given it much thought. A wife at some point. A mother."

Ben shoved his clothes back into the bag. "You dream of having a child? What about when you were six?"

"When I was six?" Iko considered as she tried on one of the white shirts over her dress. The sleeves were the right length. She'd be able to tailor it down. "I wanted to be a painter."

"Do you still paint?"

"No. I wasn't any good at it."

"Says who?"

"My teacher."

Ben snorted. "What do teachers know? I've seen your word pictures. Do that. People will love them. Well, all the good people will. They're the ones that matter. Teachers are sticks in the mud."

Iko gave him a non-committal smile and nod. She picked out one dark blue scarf and tied it around her throat like a choker. "What do you think?"

"I think it's perfect." Iko packed away the rest of Pam's scarves and belts in her trunk. Ben's eyes softened. "I hope you find a use for them. Away from here."

"I'm sure I will." She placed a hand on his arm and he jerked away.

"Sorry." She opened the white shirt, but left it on to warm her arms.

"It's okay. I've just got a bruise there."

"What happened?"

"Cop happened. Broken ribs from the same asshole who punched Pam." He winced. "Sorry about the language."

"It's okay." Iko touched his shoulder lightly. "I hope you get to see her soon."

Ben closed his eyes. "They beat me for trying to protect her. It wasn't until there was blood on the ground from the baby that they stopped. The train station paid for our tickets because we missed the first train." He took a deep breath. "Forget it. It's in the past. It's over."

He picked up his guitar and sat back down in his seat. He picked out a tune. Iko stood uncertainly in front of her trunk. She took the sketchbook out to keep with her. She flipped the little gold latches closed. She closed her eyes and dropped her chin to her chest. She took deep breaths. Tears pressed at the back of her eyes and made her cheeks and jaw ache. She took a shaky breath and moved back to her seat. "A new hand, I think."

Lewis looked up at her and nodded. "Your deal, my dear."

Nora's breath hitched. The guitar jangled to a stop. She sighed and slumped. Her breath deepened. Iko left out her breath. "I really don't know how much I can take of this."

Lewis put a hand over hers and squeeze. "One more hand, Iko."

She nodded and dealt the cards. "And one more."

He nodded. "Exactly. Tell me more about your brother."

"Oh, Jesus." Ben's voice exploded into the space. Nora flickered and disappeared before their eyes. "And then there were three." He rubbed his face and through his hair. His hair stood up in random spikes like an aggravated cat. He chewed on his lip. "Do you really think that we can make it out of this? Or should I just lie down?"

"We can make it through this." Iko's voice was stronger than she'd expected. "You will finish your song and let us hear it."

"Do you write music in traditional formats?" Lewis leaned forward.

Ben shook his head. "As soon as I'm done, I'll try to transcribe it. I don't know how well I do. I manage to get the chords written down at least. I just remember them."

"Teach it to me. I don't read music, but I used to sing at my church."

Ben patted the seat next to him. Iko joined him there. Lewis gathered her cards and dealt himself a hand of solitaire. It was Pam's song, that much was obvious. She picked up the small notebook. "Are these the words?" He nodded.

"Do you play?"

"I never have." She read through the song. "Sing it for me?"

She leaned her head against the wall of the train. It vibrated through her body. She could feel every turn of the wheels. The words of the song fell into the rhythm of the train. She nodded in time with the music. Then, she picked up the chorus easily enough. She saw Ben's face turn wistful in the reflection. She saw bruises around his eyes. She blinked and they disappeared.

"You have a lovely voice. You should keep singing," Ben said.

"Play the main melody for me?" Iko asked.

Lewis' fingers twitched as if he wanted to play. Iko ignored him until she had the melody down. Ben's smile showed a sliver of teeth. There was a gap in the front. She sang quietly until she had the melody and the lyrics in the right order.

Ben coughed suddenly, explosively. He bent over his guitar. A single drop of blood ran down the back of his hand. Lewis stiffened at the sight. He offered his silk handkerchief. "I'll ruin it." Ben shook his head.

"It's just a piece of fabric."

Ben wiped off his hand. The dark liquid soaked through quickly. It blossomed like a flower against the blue silk. Or maybe it was a cloud. Iko entertained the notion of trying to find the animals and people living in the stains. She forced her attention back to the lyrics. Ben's handwriting was surprisingly neat. The paper of his notebook was cheap. A few holes from an over-forceful stab of his pen littered the edges.

"Sing it for me once more, Iko," he said. The words forced themselves through the gasp of his breathing. His rib must have shifted to pierce his lung. Tears burned her eyes. She took a sip of water, then started to sing. As she finished, his smile was a thin, watercolor thing. It didn't suit him. "I'll write down the chords, now." He took the notebook back and noted the chords in an arcane series of letters and symbols that she couldn't identify.

She glanced over at Lewis. He was studying the newspaper intently between flicks of his eyes to Ben's hands. His fingers moved on his thigh, pressing down in a strange sort of rhythm. She was startled when Ben took the guitar off of his shoulder and held it out across the aisle.

Lewis took it as though he were handling fine china. "May I see the notebook?"

Ben smirked. "Give it a shot without it first. I want to make sure you know what you're doing."

Lewis snorted. "I'll have you know that my father played guitar. I never did get to touch his though." He seemed pensive. He bent over the instrument. His fingers caressed its neck in a way that made Iko fell that she should look away.

"Need some alone time with her?" Ben's lascivious grin was strained into more of a death's head. His skin seemed pale and there was sweat on his brow.

"I won't scandalize Miss Maynard." He paused. "Well, no more than she'd like to be."

Ben coughed out a little laugh at that. More blood-flowers blossomed onto the silk handkerchief. Iko rested her hand on his wrist. He lifted his chin, though it trembled and stared across at the other man. Lewis fingered the guitar, strumming quietly.

"All right. I'll give it a try. Let me know how much work I have to do."

It took several tries, but Ben eventually declared Lewis adequate. "Here's the chords. Iko, you sing with him. Keep him on pace." He leaned forward to touch both of them. "I need you to remember. Please."

"I do work best under pressure," Lewis informed them. He had a smile on his lips that implied a wealth of inside jokes and memories that they didn't share. He worked his way through the opening chords. Iko closed her eyes and fell into the song. Behind her eyelids she could see Pam and Ben running like children in the rain, their hair plastered down, smiling and laughing as they splashed through the puddles. The vision ended in a sweet Hollywood kiss that bought a warm smile to her face.

Ben's wrist went slack. Iko's eyes popped open. She touched his shoulder briefly, then felt for his pulse. Lewis set the guitar aside reverently. He closed his fingers over hers where they rested useless on the lifeless wrist. "I'll lay him out in the luggage room."

Iko nodded. This time she didn't bother to restrain the tears that burned in her eyes.  They slipped down her cheeks in a simple streams until the fell onto her skirt. She wiped at them with the back of her hand. The song ran through her mind again. Young love – so beautiful, so alien. She tucked his notebook into her waistband. She took up her pad and pencil and made a memorial of Ben's words and guitar.

"And then there were two," Lewis stated. He set a twist of newsprint on her lap like a flower.

She looked up sharply. "So you're suggesting we just give into whatever this is?"

"I'm suggesting that we keep our options open."

Chapter 24

Iko scrubbed at her tears with the side of her hand, smearing graphite across her cheekbone with careless precision. "What options? Do we just sit here and wait for sleep?"

"No. We go for dinner and toast to absent friends." The note of grief in his voice captured her attention.

"Yes, a toast." She stood and smoothed her skirt absently. She patted at the tendrils of hair that curled around her right ear. She tucked them back, but let the style continue to ravel. She put her purse over her shoulder and put the sketchpad in the crook of her arm.

Lewis frowned at her for a moment, then resettled his suitcoat. He patted the pocket-watch in his vest pocket. The guitar went over his shoulder. He cast his eyes around the compartment until he spotted the fedora he'd tucked into the rack under his seat.

Iko pulled on her gloves. She evaluated the reflection in the window. She looked mostly respectable. If you didn't look closely at the bruises on her face and throat. I should be able to see the difference.

"Is there anything you can't do without in your trunk?" Lewis himself was digging through his bag. He had a small gun on the floor next to him and a larger one that he'd holstered at the small of his back. He pulled out a leather holster for his ankle and a small leather case that he tucked into an inside pocket.

"Mr. Lewis, is there something I should know?" Her voice didn't waver. Her hand tightened on the sketchbook.

He  looked up, eyes going wide. He flushed. "I'm not exactly a journalist. That's always been Dom. It does let me travel almost anywhere though."

"Then what are you? A police officer?"

"I work, worked, for... the government. I haven't decided if I still work for them."

Iko stiffened her spine and pulled up the sternest face she could. It worked just as well on Mr. Lewis as it had on the children she'd looked after for the neighborhood ladies during their Bible-study meetings. He shifted uncomfortably, tugging at the bottom of his vest as he stood facing her.

"I was in France during the war. Prior to the fighting. My wife and son were killed in a raid. She was shot and died in my arms. My son... my son lasted long enough to die in a Red Cross hospital." He fiddled with the edge of his vest, the chain of his watch. "I stopped being an editor, a journalist and started being a spy. But that doesn't matter."

"They thought my mother and grandmother were spies. They put us into camps like the German Jews. My father fought in Germany and they still thought we were spies. The government is not my friend." Anger coursed through her. "What has being a spy gotten you?"

"A measure of justice." He stood tall and looked her in the eye. "And I am no longer a spy." His lips trembled a bit. He swallowed, but lifted his chin.

"Just like that?" Her eyes narrowed, but he was telling the truth. She could feel it.

"Just like that." He offered his arm. "Would you like to accompany me to dinner?"

She considered saying "no" just to see his reaction. The anger wore off. He'd fought in the war, not made decisions in some isolated Washington room. Her stomach felt sour, but she swallowed hard against it. "Yes, of course." She took the offered arm and stood straight. She painted a smile onto her face. "Some day, you'll have to tell me the real story." He huffed a small laugh.

Lewis' smile looked tired as he helped her into her seat. The waiter lit the candle in its mercury glass holder. "Would you like a bottle of wine?"

"A rose if you have it." Lewis said. "And answers if you have those." He settled the guitar in its own seat next to him. Iko laid her pad on the table and the gold pen behind her ear.

The waiter shook his head. "The wine we have. Answers? We'll see what we can do, but they're not nice."

"As long as they're true," Iko said firmly.

The man considered them for a moment. "Would you like the special? We have fish with risotto or pasta Alfredo with baked chicken?"

"I'll have the pasta," Lewis stated. "And black coffee as well as the wine."

"The fish. And tea, please." Iko folded her hands in her lap in an attempt to keep herself from fiddling with the knife. She twisted her serviette instead.

"Yes, ma'am."

The waiter moved off.

"During the war, did you have to kill?" Her mother would be appalled at the abrupt question.

"Yes." His voice was calm. "There's no shame in killing to protect yourself."

She met his eyes. "How do you bear it?"

Lewis didn't answer right away. She was content to let the question weigh down the table between them. She stared out at empty countryside as the sunset bathed the farm buildings in orange light. There were no animals in the fields only the silent sentinels of haystacks. "Not well at first." His voice was rough, full of tears or choked with regret, she couldn't tell. "I had nightmares, even waking dreams, but it was kill or be killed and eventually..." He took and uneven breath. "Eventually, I stopped thinking about it. The nightmares faded." He reached across the table carefully. "He was trying to kill you, Miss Maynard. You were completely justified."

"I know." She whispered the words to the window. She dropped her wrinkled serviette into her lap. She touched his hand as lightly as a butterfly before retreating to her own space. The arrival of dinner was a relief.

She dissected her fish into tiny mouthfuls. It tasted spectacular. It melted on her tongue and flaked off perfectly under pressure from her fork. The lemon was bright and sharp on her tongue. It should taste like ash or mud or something horrible, not fresh and perfect. She only continued to eat because stopping would lead to more discussion and that would be worse.

The waiter shepherded them through dessert and sherry and coffee before he favored them with a sympathetic smile. "The conductor will talk to you, but you'll have to go up to the engine." He shifted. "Would you like another coffee before you go?"

"Miss Maynard?"

She grimaced into her cup. She set it down carefully. It clinked in the thick white saucer. "No. Thank you."

Iko looked up into the waiter's sad smile. "Alright then." He stepped away and gave them a formal nod. Lewis nodded back. He folded his napkin into a neat square and set it in front of himself.

"If you'll excuse me for a moment."

"Of course." She smiled despite the fear that clenched her stomach, souring it even more than the coffee. The waiter cleared the table. He left a discrete package of stomach powder by her water glass. She tucked the packet into her purse. She took her turn in the bathroom. She stared into the mirror. The bruises on her throat had darkened like wooden prayer beads. The bruise on her check was too dark to cover with make-up. She sighed and pushed at her hair. It was as good as she could expect. Tendrils hung from behind her ears. She settled the little gold pen more firmly behind her ear. She looked at the gloves in her purse, but shut it with a sharp click without putting them on. No more gloves and matching hats for her.

Lewis was fingering the guitar and leaning against the wall. He didn't look like the same man, despite the suit. His face wasn't nearly as tense. "How are you so calm?" she demanded.

He looked up. His eyes were wide. He blinked. The small smile faded. "At this point, it's not worth any more worry." He shifted the guitar until it laid across his back. The strap cut across his body, pinning down his tie and marring the line of his vest. He offered his hand. "Shall we?"

She declined his hand. "Let's."

Chapter 25

Iko stood, fingers twisting together. She reached toward the door and then dropped her hand. Lewis quirked his lips. "Ladies first?"

She laughed at that. Something warm lifted in her chest. She reached out and grasped the metal handle. It was slick and cool on her palm. She yanked it open with a quick motion like pulling off a bandage. The train rocked side to side. She stared into darkness of a carriage she didn't recognize. "After you." She gave him her sweetest smile.

"Miss, wait. Your sketchbook," the waiter called.

She cradled it against her hip. "Thank you."

"Into the breach." Lewis took a deep breath. He stepped through the doorway. He absently offered his hand as they crossed the space between the cars. The carriage they entered was darker than the dining car and their usual carriage. They stood, rocking with the gentle motion of the car.

Iko's eyes adjusted to the gloom to reveal a car filled with traveling trunks of multiple stages of wear. Small soft carpet bags were stuffed on top and between them. On one side a seemingly precarious stack of hatboxes was hemmed in by a haphazard stack of winter coats and woolen blankets. The other side was a welter of boxes and bags of various shapes and sizes. A powder blue make-up case was sprawled open in the center of the aisle. Its contents spread along the bare floor like a hastily abandoned set of children's toys.

The air was dusty and full of smoke from the engine. "Was this here earlier when you..."

"No. Not like this." There was a slight tremor in his voice. He wrapped his fingers around her hand, not asking this time. His fingers were firm on hers. He gave her palm a squeeze. She wasn't sure if that were for his benefit or hers.

"Only way out is through," she murmured. She stepped forward, avoiding the scattered lipstick cases. She tugged on his hand when he didn't move.

"Dom and I came searching this way, but we couldn't get through. The train was shaking too wildly," he whispered. "He was here, wasn't he? I've pretended to be him and written unsent letters and spoken to him, but I could actually touch him."

"Yes." She didn't look back. She didn't want to embarrass him.

"Onward then." He fell into step behind her, their fingers still tangled in a way that would appall her mother. They stopped once more, staring at the next door. Lewis opened it with a quick sharp movement. The space beyond was cleaner than Iko expected. It smelled of diesel fuel and sweating male. The man at the throttle looked over his shoulder.

"I don't bite. Find a place to sit if you want."

Iko looked around then down at her skirt. "I'll stand." The vibration of the engine made the light dance across her skirt. Iko reached out to grip the shiny handle of the door, but stopped and found a piece of machinery that looked sturdy. The oil smeared across her hand. She stared at it as the lights dimmed. Lewis leaned against one of the hulking pieces of machinery. He looked almost at home there.

"So, I'm sure you kids have questions."

"Miss Maynard?"

"Oh, no, please, after you." She smiled sweetly in response to the frown he sent her way.

"What the Hell is going on here?"

The engineer laughed at them. "Less tactful than the last two who came through." He wiped away the tears of mirth. Iko's fingers clenched with familiar anger. She hated being laughed at. "You two have the chance of a lifetime or beyond. Just one last step to take."

"Meaning?" Iko's throat felt tight and her voice was harsh because of it.

"You can stay here on the train. Meet the next candidates or you can walk out that door and step off the train."

"Candidates for what?"

"For learning the truth."

Iko sighed. "The truth about what?"

"You'll find out if you step out the door." The conductor's smile was sly. "All I'll say is that it's a good thing."

"At this speed?" Lewis' shoulders straightened and his chin lifted.

"Not like it'll kill you."

"What are you talking about?"

"You step off the train, you'll understand. Stay here with us until the next ride. Pick someone who catches your eye and fade out. Or take a leap of faith."

"I have no reason to believe anything you say."

Iko stared out the blurry window. She saw, however, an old woman serving her tea. She looked down at the watch on her wrist. "Mr. Lewis," she broke into the rant. "When did Mr. Gold give you his watch?"

Lewis froze. He looked down at the pocket-watch. "It was in his will. Something to remember him by. I've been using it for years when I'm traveling as Dom." His voice was bleak. "But he was wearing it earlier, wasn't he?"

Iko nodded.

Lewis' spine stiffened. He took a breath. "It was time to let him go. I can't keep hiding behind him."

Iko smiled at that. "What will we do if we take this leap?" She regarded the engineer with a calm face that hid the over-fast beating of her heart. Her grandmother would be so pleased that she'd finally learned the trick.

"Live in the world. Help the living, the dying. Change the world or maybe settle down and have a family. I don't know. Just that it's your choice to make. A second chance. And when you finally decide it's time to pass on, you'll know how to find your way back here. Or you can just stay. Keep riding until the next group of candidates comes along. The chef'd be pleased to have you to cook for."

"Candidates," Lewis murmured. He ran the chain of the pocket-watch through his fingers. He seemed lost in his head. "Who chose Nora? Who chose a little girl for this? Is it because she was dying? Who chose any of us?"

The engineer shifted. The train seemed to edge forward just a bit more. "I ain't got those sort of answers. I just drive the train. Unless one of you kids wants to take over?" He wiped at the back of his neck with a blue handkerchief.

"Who chose us?" Lewis leaned forward, trying to be threatening.

"Ben and Pam, of course. Good kids. Snuck on board in New Orleans a few years ago. Put off dyin' until they found someone to carry on their work."

"Years ago? How long have we been on this train?" Lewis demanded.

"You two, not long. They could only choose from soon to be dead folks though."

"Soon to be dead?" Iko swallowed hard. "How was I..." She put a hand to her throat and felt the echos of the scarf twisting and cutting off her air; Serendinski holding the ends of it and dropping her to the floor as she choked. She shook it off. He was dealt with.

Lewis was still. "I was actually going to do it then," he said quietly.

The conductor shifted from foot to foot and opened the throttle further. "Going to? Son, you did. Shot yourself right in the noggin before we left DC." The train rocked faster and faster.

She was dead. She would stay here until she chose someone else or... She couldn't stay on this train one more minute and she couldn't continue on to Boston. She wasn't the Iko who'd started this journey. She didn't need vengance anymore.

Ben's song echoed in Iko's ears. The song of life. She clutched the notebook and her purse to her side. She yanked open the door and threw herself out toward the tracks. She heard a fractured "Iko!" The wind caught her and she closed her eyes. Her skirt wrapped around her legs, but she didn't hit the ground. It was like falling in a dream. She opened her eyes and saw blue beneath her, then colors. Colors she'd never seen and couldn't name surrounded her. They twisted around and over her like scarves or smoke. She smelled home – her mother's kitchen, her grandmother's liniment, the cherry blossoms near the Potomac, her father's cigars, her brother's model glue. Like the ringing of a deep clear bell everything made perfect sense. She felt a weight lift off of her. Her memories were once again sharp.

The song. She had to preserve the song. As long as the music survived, so did love.

That feeling dissipated as she landed, or rather she came back to herself, standing at the back of a gawking crowd. The notebook was clutched tightly in her chest and there was oil smeared on her hand. The train was laying on its side. People were rushing to help the people stumbling out of the broken train. Her eyes were drawn to a little girl in her mother's arms. She was dry-eyed but clung to her mother with white knuckles. "Nora," she whispered. "Oh thank God." Hopefully all of the sleepers were alive.

She swallowed, then turned away from the wreck. The sight of a guitar slung over a retreating shoulder made her breath catch. "Mr. Lewis!" She jogged up to him. She offered his pen. "I forgot to return your pen."

When their eyes met she could see the awful, wonderful knowledge in his eyes. "Please keep it." He angled his body to look away from the train. "Ben and Pam were just found," he murmured. "Their bodies, I mean."

She winced. She knew they were out of pain now, but it still hurt. She took a breath to steady herself. "I should call my father." She made no move to find a phone or a telegraph.

"I'm not going back to the OSS," Lewis said quietly. "I'll be Lewis Gold now. If you, if you happen to see my byline."

"I'll look for it. The New York papers."

They watched as Serendinski was led away from the train in handcuffs. "Do you know what happened?" She nodded toward her killer.

"Police were looking for a murderer. Killed several woman and was escaping on the train." He looked at her for a moment. "I saw them taking a body away." He stopped. "Mine. I'm pretty sure if you look to your right, over by the bathrooms, you'll see yours."

Iko pulled herself up straight. "That doesn't matter. That life is over. At least I saw my family once more."

Lewis nodded. He seemed younger than when they'd met. "You're off to Boston then," he said.

The very idea of becoming someone's assistant again, finding a husband, becoming a responsible, quiet young woman who was a credit to her family made her stomach twist. She nodded. "I should. I should find a way to get there." She fiddled with the gold pen. Ben's song echoed in her ears.

His eyes flicked from her face to the sketchbook and then to the train. He swallowed, then straightened his shoulders. He gave her a smile and a nod. He touched the strap of the guitar. "Did you... Nevermind."

She nodded back and turned to walk away. Four slow steps later he spoke.

"Miss Maynard, I seem to be lacking a traveling partner."

She turned. "I think I might find myself in need of an adventure."

The smile he gave her reminded her of Mr. Gold. He offered his arm. "Miss Maynard, would you do me the honor of accompanying me?"

"Iko, please. Iko Shiro." The new name settled around her like the rook she'd named herself after. She'd remember Pam every day now. "I think we need to practice a bit don't you, Mr. Gold?"

"Songs are meant to be shared. Where shall we head, Miss Shiro?"

She looked at the train as it lay on its side.

"Anywhere that we don't need a train to get to."

Lewis laughed, and she heard music.

The End

# ABOUT THE AUTHOR

*Kate Ressman has been writing for her entire life. It's true—she has proof of a second grade story where a cat inherits his human's money. A bit of a nomad in the past, she has settled down and currently lives in Northern Virginia. She has two businesses, a day job, and an imaginary cat.*

www.ingramcontent.com/pod-product-compliance
Lightning Source LLC
Chambersburg PA
CBHW051258210726
48287CB00002B/556